THE CHRONICLES OF Vladimir Tod

NINTH GRADE SLAYS

Heather Brewer

speak

An Imprint of Penguin Group (USA) Inc.

SPEAK

Published by the Penguin Group

Penguin Group (USA) Inc., 345 Hudson Street, New York, New York 10014, U.S.A.

Penguin Group (Canada), 90 Eglinton Avenue East, Suite 700, Toronto, Ontario, Canada M4P 2Y3
(a division of Pearson Penguin Canada Inc.)

Penguin Books Ltd, 80 Strand, London WC2R 0RL, England

Penguin Ireland, 25 St Stephen's Green, Dublin 2, Ireland (a division of Penguin Books Ltd)

Penguin Group (Australia), 250 Camberwell Road, Camberwell, Victoria 3124, Australia
(a division of Pearson Australia Group Pty Ltd)

Penguin Books India Pvt Ltd, 11 Community Centre, Panchsheel Park, New Delhi - 110 017, India

Penguin Group (NZ), 67 Apollo Drive, Rosedale, North Shore 0632, New Zealand
(a division of Pearson New Zealand Ltd.)

Penguin Books (South Africa) (Pty) Ltd, 24 Sturdee Avenue,
Rosebank, Johannesburg 2196, South Africa

Registered Offices: Penguin Books Ltd, 80 Strand, London WC2R 0RL, England

First published in the United States of America by Dutton Children's Books,
a division of Penguin Young Readers Group, 2008
Published by Speak, an imprint of Penguin Group (USA) Inc., 2009

5 7 9 10 8 6 4

CIP Data is available.

ISBN: 978-0-525-47892-8 (hc)

Speak ISBN 978-0-14-241342-5

Designed by Jason Henry
Printed in the United States of America

▼ ▼ ▼

*This one's for Jacob,
because high school sucks*

——————— ACKNOWLEDGMENTS ———————

Books may be written by writers, but they are perfected by an entire range of people who don't receive the amount of praise they should. I'd like to thank my amazing editor, Maureen Sullivan, for working tirelessly to push me into bettering my craft, and for always having insightful ideas and a positive attitude. Thanks to everyone at Dutton, simply for doing everything that they can to make my dream a reality. Special thanks to my incredibly talented cover designer, Christian Funfhausen, for giving me the most kick-butt smiley a vampire author could ever want. And I owe an enormous amount of gratitude to my fabulous agent, Michael Bourret, for always giving me your shoulder, your eyes, your ears, and your brilliance. Without all of you, I'm just a hack with a keyboard and a thirst for blood.

Many, many thanks to the most amazing critique partner a girl can have—Jackie Kessler, who never fails to amaze me with her skill and is quick with the sympathetic chocolates. Thanks, also, to my sister, Dawn Vanniman, for believing in me and for continuing to love Seth. And, of course, thanks to Paul, Jacob, and Alexandria—I don't know how, but "you people" managed to stay out of my way long enough for me to write another book, and I love you for it.

Thanks also to the future keepers of the Brewtopian kingdom, to my loyal Minion Horde, to every bookseller and librarian that has introduced Vlad to readers . . . and to you, the person holding this book, for giving Vlad a chance, and for following him into his high school years.

Vlad and I couldn't do it without you.

Contents

1	HUNTER FOR HIRE	3
2	THE HUNGER	5
3	BATHORY HIGH	20
4	*PSYCHO SLASHER CHAIN-SAW GUY FROM HELL*	42
5	KILLER AT LARGE	50
6	HALLOWEEN	54
7	AN UNEXPECTED INVITATION	71
8	SECRETS EXPOSED	89
9	SNOWFLAKES AND MEMORIES	99
10	SIBERIA	113
11	VIKAS	121
12	HONORING TOMAS TOD	135
13	MIND CONTROL	143
14	TRAINING INTERRUPTED	162
15	WHERE THE HEART IS	177
16	THE HEALING POWER OF BLOOD	190
17	TRAPPED	195
18	THE FRIEND CODE	204
19	A SON'S DUTY	217
20	AN ENEMY REVEALED	228
21	*ET TU, JOSS?*	238
22	THE AFTERLIFE	259
23	THE SILVER LINING	275

The Chronicles of Vladimir Tod

NINTH GRADE SLAYS

1
HUNTER FOR HIRE

JASIK GRIPPED THE PHOTOGRAPH in his hand and scanned the face of the boy. Except for his pale complexion and clever eyes, no one would suspect the teen was anything other than human. But Jasik knew differently.

"This is him, then?" He looked up to the man behind the desk, who nodded once.

"Vladimir Tod." The man's voice was hoarse and raspy.

Jasik slipped the photo into his shirt pocket and cleared his throat against his fist. "I will need provisions, of course."

"I will provide whatever you need." The man wore a bitter, pinched expression on his face.

Jasik crossed the room and looked out the window to the city streets outside. It was dark, despite the many streetlights. People moved like ants on the pavement below, avoiding the small pools of light. There was almost no telling which were human and which vampires. Jasik wondered briefly if the sun suddenly rose and bathed them all in light, whether they would scurry away and seek their darkness elsewhere. "Might I ask how you came to know of my services?"

The man behind the desk coughed into a handkerchief before answering. When he removed the cloth from his lips, it was stained with glistening red. "Let's not play games, Jasik. I've known for many years that your . . . talents . . . can be bought. Will you hunt this boy, or not?"

Jasik glanced back at the man and smirked. "My talents are expensive."

"I assure you, there is no price that I am unwilling to pay."

The man behind the desk leaned forward and flipped open his checkbook. After scribbling for a moment, he paused and nodded to Jasik. "All you need to do is provide me with the number of zeros."

Jasik faced the desk and glimpsed the check. The ink had not yet dried before he said, "Three more and you've got a deal."

2
THE HUNGER

VLAD SQUEEZED HIS EYES shut tight. He was awake, but he wasn't incredibly happy about it. Weekends, even summer weekends, were meant for sleeping in . . . especially when those weekends were spent hanging out super late under the full moon because your vampire genes won't let you go to bed before they've had their fill of nighttime. Even more so when you only had a matter of days before the joy of summer would be over and the dread of school would begin.

A low, buzzing sound drifted over his face, paused, then moved again toward his right ear. He popped open one eye and glared in disgust at the housefly that was hovering about the room. So that's what had woken him.

The fly fluttered over and landed on the tip of Vlad's nose. He swatted it away, and when it took refuge on his pillow, he smacked his hand down to squash it, but missed. Vlad grumbled obscenities under his breath. What did the fly have against sleep, anyway?

Flapping its tiny wings, it buzzed across the room and landed directly on the center of Henry's forehead.

After a moment of hesitation, Vlad crept over to Henry's sleeping bag. He raised his hand slowly, giving the fly one final chance to move. He whispered, "Don't think I won't do it."

The fly responded by washing its gross little fly face. If it could have spoken, Vlad was almost positive it would have laughed at him.

Vlad brought his hand down fast and hard. The slapping sound his palm made when it hit Henry's skin echoed throughout his bedroom but was shortly covered by a yelp from Henry, who sat up, clutching his forehead. "Dude!"

Vlad straightened his shoulders, triumphant in battle. "There was a fly."

Henry rubbed his forehead, snarling in disgust. "Well, did you at least kill it?"

"Yeah, I think so."

The fly buzzed past his ear and out the door.

Vlad swore again but was cut off by Henry. "I smell bacon."

But it wasn't the smell of bacon that called to Vlad. It was the promise of a steamy mug of O positive and a gooey cinnamon roll, Aunt Nelly's specialty. One big plus of living with Nelly—who was actually no relation to him at all, but his mother's best friend for years and years before his parents had passed on—was that she could bake cinnamon rolls so sweet and delicious that if she had the determination and funding, she could easily give Cinnabon a run for their money. Just stay away from her meat loaf.

They raced out the door and down the stairs. By the time they reached the kitchen, they were panting and famished. Henry spotted the plate of crisp bacon on the table and grunted. "Food."

Vlad opened the freezer and grabbed a bag of blood. He plucked a coffee mug from the cupboard and nudged Henry out of the way as he headed for the microwave. "Food."

Aunt Nelly turned from her spot at the stove and chuckled. "I take it that means you boys are hungry?"

But neither Vlad nor Henry answered with any sound that could be classified as a yes or a no. Henry was too busy chewing on several slices of bacon at once, and Vlad had his head tilted back as he gulped down some warm O positive. It slid down his throat easily—it was always better warm—and when his thirst was quenched, he smacked his lips in satisfaction and reached for a cinnamon roll.

Blood and frosting: the vampire's answer to coffee and donuts.

"Deb mentioned that an entire freezer of blood is about to expire at the hospital. With your appetite lately, Vladimir,

I'd better sneak out as much of it as I can." Nelly placed more bacon on the platter and sat a plate of eggs in front of Henry. She flashed Vlad a look of disapproval. "You've got blood all over your shirt."

Vlad looked down at the two dime-size red circles on his shirt and smiled sheepishly. "Sorry. I was really hungry."

Nelly's gaze softened. "Just be more careful next time. Contrary to popular belief, laundry doesn't top my list of favorite things to do."

Henry swallowed and reached for the pitcher of orange juice. "So did you get your schedule yet?"

Vlad nodded and sighed with an air of gloom and doom. "I got Mrs. Bell for English, first period."

Henry offered Vlad a sympathetic glance. "Looks like you're not alone. I've got her, too, and from what my mom said yesterday, so does Joss."

"When's your cousin supposed to get here anyway?" Vlad stuffed most of the gooey cinnamon roll into his mouth and chewed. The truth was he was kind of nervous about Henry's cousin moving to town. There was always the slight chance that Joss would interfere with his and Henry's time together, or worse, that he and Joss might not get along.

"Sunday. Oh, and just so you know, don't count on seeing me much that day. My mom's on some family togetherness kick." Henry rolled his eyes.

Vlad followed suit. "How annoying."

Nelly flashed him an incredulous glance. "Vladimir!"

Vlad took a sip of blood and raised an eyebrow at Henry. "I mean, how lovely of your parental figure to insist on enjoying quality time together. You should be grateful."

Both boys broke into hysterical laughter. Nelly chuckled and shook her head. "All right, smart mouth. I'm getting the mail. Henry, watch Vlad while I'm gone. He's a trouble-maker."

Vlad's jaw dropped in mock exasperation. "Nelly!"

Nelly smiled sweetly. "I mean, he's a wonderful boy who brightens my day and makes life worth living."

After she slipped out the front door, Vlad eyed the wicked glimmer in Henry's eye suspiciously. "What?"

Henry's grin broadened. "Did you call Meredith yet?"

Vlad straightened his shoulders proudly. "Twice, actually."

Henry watched him for a moment, the surprise in his eyes quickly giving way to suspicion. "You talked to her?"

Talk to her? Vlad hadn't yet figured out a way to remove the lump that had taken up residence in his throat ever since she'd leaned in for a kiss after the Freedom Fest dance and he'd backed away, babbling like some kind of deranged lunatic. Talking to her was the least of his problems. First he needed to figure out how to breathe whenever she was near.

Vlad slowly stretched his hand out and picked up his mug, then took a long drink before returning it to the table.

When he was finished, he met Henry's eyes and sighed. "Nope. Hung up both times. I think she heard me breathing once though."

"That's progress." Henry sighed. "You know she has caller ID, right?"

Vlad's eyes grew wide. There it was again, that lump in his throat. "She does?"

Henry answered with a tone of indifference. "Yeah. But dude, check this out." He grinned wickedly and lowered his voice to a tone of conspiracy. "Last night, Greg told me something interesting about the upperclassmen girls."

Vlad leaned up against the counter and tried to act like he wasn't completely curious. "Interesting? Like how?"

Henry leaned closer. "He says that if you can get invited to one of the senior parties, that some of those girls take pity on the lower classmen and they'll—"

Aunt Nelly walked into the kitchen. In one hand was a stack of envelopes, in the other was a small brown box. She glanced at their frozen, startled expressions and raised an eyebrow. "What are you boys talking about?"

They answered in one wavering voice, "Nothing!"

Vlad eyed the envelopes hopefully. "Anything from Otis?"

Nelly sighed and shook her head as she flipped through the stack. "Honestly, Vladimir. Your uncle has written to you at least once a week since the day he left Bathory. Do you really think he'd forget about you now?" She pulled a thick parchment envelope from the pile and held it out to him with a smile.

Vlad sighed in relief. He'd only just met his uncle last year, after a horrible misunderstanding. Vlad had no idea Otis was his uncle at the time, instead believing him to be a maniacal substitute teacher, out to expose Vlad's secret and quite possibly kill him. It was a simple mistake—anyone could have made it. Instead, Otis had been protecting him from D'Ablo, the president of an Elysian council, who was determined to find Vlad and punish him for the crime of existing.

Apparently, vampires aren't really big on the idea of humans and vampires having kids together.

Ever since Otis had left town in order to flee from Elysia and away from vampirekind, Vlad and Otis had exchanged many letters. In them, Otis had taught him how to read the vampiric language, otherwise known as Elysian code, and had urged him to practice his telepathy daily. Vlad was grateful for all of these things.

Of course, Otis had also recently encouraged Vlad to work on controlling the minds of others. Vlad was intrigued—there was no doubt about that. But there was one aspect that Otis hadn't thought about. What if Vlad got caught? The ability to control the thoughts and actions of other people could hardly be blamed on your normal, everyday teenage hormones.

Still . . . it might make algebra easier to pass.

But rather than explain his fear of being discovered, Vlad had written his uncle several weeks ago and insisted that he was incapable of controlling the minds of others, hoping that Otis would accept it as a lost cause and move on to some of the stealthier abilities of the undead. Like animorphing . . . or maybe luring females with a glance.

He tore open the envelope and after squinting at Otis's crooked handwriting for a moment—it always took him some time to adjust his eyes—he read.

Dearest Vladimir,

I hope this letter finds you well. To answer your most recent questions: (1) No, there has been no further word from Elysia concerning you or your father. However, you must remember that I am no longer privileged to information concerning the legal procedures of the Stokerton council. All of my information is hearsay and, therefore, not completely reliable. (2) Your aunt is right to be so "overprotective" and insist that you go nowhere alone. You may be a fearsome creature of the night, Vladimir, but you are also a teenager and, by definition, her ward. Besides, it is possible that Elysia may decide to exact vengeance for your murder of their president last year . . . despite the fact that it was self-defense. (3) I'm sorry, Vladimir, but the rumor that vampires are able to charm women with a leering gaze is utterly ridiculous and completely false. Have you tried simply asking Meredith if she likes you? In my experience, the direct approach works best. Calling a girl and breathing into the phone never got anyone a date. Whatever you decide, remember to be a gentleman.

As promised, I am enclosing further instructions on how to best develop your telepathic skills. It surprises me that you have had only minimal success with this trait, as you should be able to read the minds of anyone you wish, but we must both remember that you are the first of your kind, Vladimir, and things will likely be different for you. When vampires are made, there is a natural order to their skill development, but you . . . you were born, and as such, we cannot be certain which traits you will inherit from your father's vampire nature, and which you will not, due to your mother's human DNA. We must deal with each of these skills as it presents itself.

Follow the enclosed instructions and practice, practice, practice! However, as your former teacher, I must insist that you refrain from using your telepathy as a means to better grades. And yes, I'll know. Trust me.

As for the issues you seem to be having with mind control, give me time to compose some helpful tips regarding this skill. Together, we'll find a way to make this possible. Your father was quite adept at doing this. I confess that it surprises me that you may not be. But please know that I am not disappointed in the least.

You are always in my thoughts, Vlad. Please take care of yourself. Be mindful of your surroundings, and please continue to study Elysian code. I know the vampire language is challenging to read, but it is important that you memorize the Compendium of Conscentia. *According to the phrase coined by the notable human philosopher George Santayana, "Those who cannot remember the past are condemned to repeat it."*

Next week I will be in London—the address where I can be reached is enclosed. I will write as often as I am able to. Please give my warm regards to Nelly.

Yours in Eternity,
Otis

Vlad ran his fingers over Otis's closing. *Yours in Eternity.* It was the same closing his dad had used in every note, every book, every birthday card, he'd ever given to Vlad. Vlad felt the looming shadow of grief sweep over him again. The death of a loved one is funny like that. It doesn't matter how much you grieve or how much time has passed, the littlest reminder of the person who died—a scent, an object, a word—can send you back to the moment you lost them, and before you can blink, you're overcome by the aching sadness you worked so hard to leave behind.

It was pretty disheartening to learn that dueling to the death last year against D'Ablo might set vampire society on his heels, despite the fact that D'Ablo had started the whole mess in the first place and Vlad had only blown a hole through him with the Lucis to avoid having D'Ablo rip one through him with his bare hands. But Vlad could deal with that. After all, thanks to Otis, Elysia thought Vlad was human, not half-vampire. Of course, Otis had said that what with Vlad possessing the Lucis, the most dangerous weapon against vampirekind, Elysia was pretty anxious to agree that he was human, to deny the notion that he was even remotly capable of hurting them, giving them little reason to chase after Vlad.

It was frustrating to learn that his uncle had absolutely no sensible advice regarding Vlad's current situation with the girl he liked. He thought about asking Nelly for her input, but the last thing he needed was a two-hour conversation about when Nelly was a teenager.

Vlad sighed. It was hopeless. How was he ever going to explain to Meredith that he had no idea why he hadn't kissed her after Freedom Fest dance last year, and that the only reason he hadn't returned her calls over the summer was that she would ask him to explain his inaction . . . and he couldn't. How was he supposed to explain something to her that even he didn't understand?

"What did he say?" Henry peered over Vlad's shoulder at the parchment.

Vlad folded the letter and shoved it back in the envelope, then withdrew the instructions. "He says to tell Nelly hi and that he's enclosed some tips on telepathy."

Nelly smiled warmly and blushed, then glanced at her watch and sighed. She shook her head and reached for her purse. On her way out the door, she called behind her, "I'm late. I was supposed to take Deb's shift at the hospital this afternoon. Can you boys fend for dinner?"

The door closed before they could answer.

Henry nodded toward Otis's instructions. "You wanna try something out? I've been dying to know if Melissa Hart likes me."

Vlad folded the notes up and slipped them in his back jeans pocket. "I want to study the notes first for a few days. Maybe we'll try something this weekend."

Henry groaned. "Come on! I'm busy this weekend. Joss, remember?"

"I want to read them first."

"So read them. Then we can head over to the mall in Stokerton. Melissa is doing that 'end of summer/fall fashion' show they do every year, and you—"

"Henry, I said no." Vlad's eyes were fixed on Henry. His tone was stern.

Henry nodded slowly and reached for his orange juice.

Drudge or not, Vlad hated giving Henry direct orders, and he only did it if Henry was being too pushy about something Vlad didn't feel like doing or discussing . . . or if Vlad really wanted a Pepsi, but he really didn't feel like going into the kitchen to get one. Other than that, their vampire/vampire's-human-slave relationship was working out pretty well. It was astounding how well Henry had taken the news that with one bite, he'd become Vlad's drudge.

But then, maybe Henry had only taken it so well because Vlad had told him to.

The thought made Vlad shiver. He didn't like the idea of controlling Henry's actions. Truthfully, it creeped him out a little. But sometimes Henry could be so pushy.

Vlad flipped over the box and, spying his name on the label, proceeded to pop the flaps open. His lips spread into a grin, and he looked at Henry. "You wanna play *Race to Armageddon 2?*"

Henry gasped at the game box in Vlad's hands. "No way!"

Vlad flipped the game over and looked at the screen shots. "They say it's twice the action, three times the gore."

Exchanging maniacal grins, they bolted for the living room.

Two hours, a bag of Doritos, seven Pepsis, and four bags of blood later, Vlad and Henry sat their controllers down and stretched. Henry's eyes were wide with awed disgust. "That's so gross. I love it!"

"No doubt. It's so cool that the androids can fly now." Vlad drained his Pepsi and sat the empty can on the coffee table. His stomach rumbled.

Henry furrowed his brow. "What's with the alien king having six heads? That's new. He's gonna be tough to beat this time."

"They really added a lot of blood. Speaking of which . . ." Vlad retrieved another bag of blood from the refrigerator. As he was walking back into the living room, he let his fangs elongate—his hunger was pulsing beneath them. He bit through the bag and drained it, then let out a burp and wiped the excess from the corners of his mouth.

Henry chuckled. "Pig."

Vlad snickered. " 'Scuse me."

Henry bit his lip thoughtfully for a moment. His tone became careful and serious. "Do you think you'll ever start feeding on people?"

Vlad shook his head. "No way. Not in a million years." He eyed Henry for a moment with his peripheral vision before facing him. "You actually think I'd do that?"

"Well, you *did* bite me when we were eight."

Vlad flashed Henry an incredulous look. "Dude, we were *eight*. Besides, you told me to."

Henry pretended not to hear him. "And just now, before you bit into that bag, your eyes changed that weird irides-cent purple the way they do when you touch a glyph." Henry nodded to the strange symbol on the cover of the

Encyclopedia Vampyrica and shrugged. "I'm just saying it's possible. I mean, what if the bags and snack packs aren't enough anymore?"

Vlad shook his head and pressed his lips tightly together, tracing the glyphlike tattoo on the inside of his left wrist lightly. There was a long moment of silence before he spoke. "If they were good enough for my dad to live on, they're good enough for me. Besides, the day I start feeding on people is the day I start beating you at video games."

Henry laughed and picked up his controller. "So you're saying it'll never happen."

3

BATHORY HIGH

VLAD SHOVED TWO PENS into the front pocket of his backpack and zipped it closed. Henry had tried convincing
him over the summer to buy a new bag, specifically a cool
coffin-shaped one they'd seen at the mall in Stokerton, but
Vlad preferred his old one. He wasn't against the gag—in
fact, he found it quite hilarious that he and Henry would
make such obvious statements about his being a vampire
and that everyone in the town of Bathory shrugged it off,
presuming Vlad to be just another goth kid—but he and his
backpack had been through two years together. It had been
up the flagpole almost as many times as Vlad had been

shoved against a locker. In a way, it was his friend. Like Henry.

If he could strap Henry to his back and force him to carry his books.

Vlad pinned a new button to his backpack and swung it over his shoulder. Seeing it in the store had sent him into a hysterical fit, so he knew Henry would love it. The pin read CAREFUL, I BITE.

Aunt Nelly's voice drifted up the stairs. "You'd better hurry or you'll be late for your first day!"

Vlad started to slip the small black cylinder into his back pocket and paused, then placed the Lucis on his dresser. He knew Otis and Nelly would freak out about him not carrying the vampire weapon for even a day, but he wasn't exactly sure what effect it might have on humans, and the idea of carrying it into class made him feel a little queasy. Weapons, even vampire weapons, had no place at school.

He took the stairs by two and flashed a smile at his aunt at the bottom.

Nelly smiled back and handed him a snack pack, which he slurped down with glee. The blood was warm and gooey and slid down his throat with ease. The breakfast of champions, indeed.

Vlad handed the plastic container back to Nelly and had just brushed the tips of his fingers against the doorknob when Nelly asked, "Did you remember to put your sunblock on?"

Vlad chuckled, resisting the urge to roll his eyes. "Why do you ask? Am I getting too tan?"

Nelly shook her head, a bemused smile on her lips, and Vlad slipped out the door.

Henry was standing on the sidewalk across the street, waiting. A bronze-skinned, good-looking kid stood next to him, and Vlad could tell by the similar facial features that they were related. Vlad gave a nod to Henry. "Hey."

Henry beamed and nodded toward the newcomer. "Hey. This is my cousin Joss."

Joss smiled but didn't say anything. Oh good. The strong, silent type.

They trudged toward the school together, following beaten paths between houses and worrying aloud about their impending first day as high schoolers. Vlad's heart was hammering its objections against his ribs. And just as he'd taken enough deep breaths to calm the beating in his chest, he rounded the corner to face the front steps of Bathory High.

Bathory High School was quite a source of gossip in the small town of Bathory, as it had once been a Catholic church. The church had been deserted sometime in the mid-1800s, due to some sort of horrific affair that no one in town—including the librarian, who knew everything about Bathory's history and seemed to take great joy in sharing it with everyone—would talk about. Nearly a hundred years later, a wealthy businessman had purchased the property and developed it into what had been known as Bathory Preparatory Academy. Twenty years after that, the school had been turned into a public institution and eventually became what Vlad was squinting up at as he approached with his backpack slung over his shoulder.

"Henry!" Carrie Anderson waved her hand enthusiastically through the air.

Henry smiled sheepishly. "Be right back, guys." In a moment, he was enveloped by a wave of the kind of popularity that Vlad had only managed to witness from the shore.

Vlad sighed and turned to Joss. "Henry says you moved in from Cali."

Joss nodded. "He tells me you suck at video games."

After a moment, they both burst into laughter. Vlad beamed. "He's a funny guy."

"Popular, too, it seems." The look on Joss's face was one of disdain.

Vlad raised a surprised eyebrow at him. "I assumed all McMillans were popular."

"Not me, man. Not my thing." Joss shook his head, casting an unsettled glance at the crowd. "I prefer a select group of friends—generally people who don't suck up to you because of who your family is or how much money they have."

Vlad smiled. He and Joss were going to get along just fine.

Henry waved, and before Joss was swallowed up by the throng, Joss adjusted the messenger bag on his shoulder and smiled at Vlad. "Well . . . see ya, I guess."

"See ya." Vlad watched Joss disappear into the crowd and turned to squint up at the school again.

But he didn't squint for long.

As hands gripped his shirt and yanked him to the side of the building, Vlad's eyes widened in fear.

Bill Jensen and Tom Gaiber. Just his luck.

They hated him and had ever since the first grade for no particular reason as far as Vlad could tell.

Together, Bill and Tom slammed Vlad against the school's stone wall, their mouths distorted into wicked grins. Tom snarled, "Welcome to your first day of high school, goth boy."

Vlad winced as his head bounced off the wall. He tried to keep his eyes glazed with indifference, but they betrayed him by flitting back to the sidewalk for any sign of help. He was about to have his face pounded into hamburger. Where was Henry when he needed him?

Bill leaned close. His breath smelled like tuna fish and three-day-old mayonnaise. "What's the matter, goth boy? Cat got your tongue?"

Several witty retorts flitted through Vlad's mind, but he thought better of saying anything and kept his mouth shut.

Sometimes your best defense against bullies is silence.

Of course, if you let a bully push you around, you're nothing but a total wuss. Straightening his shoulders, Vlad shoved back against Bill, but Tom grabbed him by the collar. A pain shot through Vlad's back as he returned forcefully to the wall.

"Let him go."

Vlad turned his head toward the sidewalk. Joss had apparently ducked away from Henry's entourage and was looking at Bill and Tom matter-of-factly. His head was tilted slightly and one of his eyebrows was raised, as if he wasn't used to people not doing what he told them to.

Apparently, Henry's cousin was funny, but not terribly bright. Vlad wanted to tell Joss to beat it, but just then Tom rolled his eyes and pushed Vlad harder against the wall. Vlad's spine was lodged against a rather pointy stone. He winced and fought to get away, but Tom had him pinned. "You're gonna get it this year, goth boy. We've got plans for you."

"I said, let him go." Joss had sat his bag on the sidewalk and was looking at Tom without so much as a glimmer of fear in his eyes.

Tom and Bill released Vlad and turned to the new-comer.

Run, Vlad thought, *run for your life, Joss. Trust me.*

Tom and Bill exchanged glances that said that they weren't really sure whether Joss was easy prey or not. With a final, deciding shove from Tom, they slinked back toward the front of the school without another word.

Vlad wondered what it was about Joss that had made them back off so quickly. Whatever it was, Vlad certainly didn't have it.

He picked up his backpack and rubbed the lump on the back of his head thoughtfully. He wasn't exactly sure how he felt about being rescued, but it was better than getting pummeled, he supposed. "Thanks."

Joss smiled. "No problem. Those guys were jerks. Brainless Neanderthal jerks."

"You've met them already?"

"Didn't need to. I could tell by their sloped foreheads and unibrows." Joss smirked. "Want me to break their arms off for you?"

Vlad chuckled. "That might be nice. I'd like to see them try to bully me then. What could they do, bump into me until it got really annoying?"

Crossing behind Joss on the sidewalk was Meredith Brookstone, dressed in a pink dress that swished about her knees as she walked. Her cheeks blushed slightly as she smiled at Vlad. Joss followed Vlad's eyes, and when he saw Meredith, he smiled, too.

Uh-oh.

Henry rejoined them and looked up at the building. "Kinda scary, isn't it?"

Vlad nodded, looking at the building looming in front of them. He'd been here a hundred times before, but what felt welcoming under a moonlit glow was about as creepy as you can get in full sunlight.

Vlad followed Henry and Joss up the steps. It felt strange to be approaching the school from the front. He kept his head down and tried not to look up at the belfry.

A sign on the door directed freshmen to the gym. Adjusting his backpack into a more comfortable position on his shoulder, Vlad took a deep breath and walked into the school.

Along either side of the lobby were thirteen large stone pillars, with arches between each at the top. Above them, on the second floor, were another, smaller set of arches. Black wrought iron closed off the top set. Vlad looked up at the high ceiling. It had clearly been painted at one time, perhaps with images of men in flowing robes and golden rings around their heads. But all that remained now were faded flecks of paint, only vaguely pictures. Several dark stones formed the shape of crosses high above Vlad's head.

Henry nudged him and whispered so that no one else would hear. "So is there any truth to the old vampires-hate-crosses myth?"

Vlad chuckled. He'd never really considered the possibility that he would burst into flames the moment he encountered a cross. In truth, he never really thought about any religion at all, one way or another. "Guess not."

A large, burly man who reminded Vlad of a giant leprechaun held up his arms and spoke in a loud, gruff, no-nonsense tone. "Freshmen, you will make your way beneath the third arch to my right and down the hall to the gym. Hurry now. Everyone else, get to class. Stevenson, that means you!"

Vlad felt a hand pat him roughly on the back and turned his head to see Greg, Henry's older brother. Greg smiled. "Don't mind Mr. Hunjo. He's always like that. You know where you're going?"

Vlad nodded and looked around for Henry and Joss, who had apparently disappeared. "Hey, where'd your brother and cousin go?"

"Probably the gym. Look for me in fourth period lunch, okay? I'll show you guys the ropes, and make sure the upperclassmen know to leave you alone." Greg patted his back again and disappeared into the crowd. Vlad watched until he could no longer see the black wool and crimson leather of Greg's letterman jacket. Greg had been the starting pitcher for the Bathory Bats for the past two years, and you could be sure that once baseball season rolled around in the spring, he'd take that position again.

Greg was quite possibly the coolest guy in existence and the only person, besides Henry, who ever made Vlad wish his parents had given him a brother. Like Henry, everybody wanted to be near Greg. You'd think that would make him obnoxious, but it didn't. He set the standard for what cool was in Bathory High.

Vlad walked under the arch and followed the flow of hesitant freshmen into the gym. The gym looked pretty much like the junior high's gymnasium, but for the large wooden beams lining the ceiling. Three tables had been set up along one wall. Vlad followed the crowd from one to the next, and when he walked out of the gym, he held a map, a school guidebook, and an assigned locker number, 131. He found his locker just down the hall, and beside it, Henry.

Henry grinned and, in his best Mister Rogers voice, said, "Hi there, neighbor. How cool is it that our lockers are right next to each other?"

"Seriously cool." Vlad pulled a red padlock out of his backpack and hooked it on the handle of his open locker. He slipped a notebook and a pen out of his bag and dropped the bag into the bottom of his locker. He was closing the door when a flash of pink caught his eye, and he turned his head.

Meredith was standing at an open locker, brushing a strand of chocolate brown hair behind her ear before hanging her pink backpack carefully inside the locker. Vlad felt his heart swell up to the size of a football. It had become so big, in fact, that he feared his chest might burst open right then and there.

Henry said, "Are you going to say hello or just stand here staring and drooling all over your shoes?"

Vlad shot him a look but didn't reply. The fact was that he wasn't sure if "hello" would be enough. He thought "sorry" might be more appropriate, but exactly what was he sorry for? For not kissing the prettiest girl in school when she kindly went with him to the last dance of the year? Absolutely. But somehow Vlad doubted that "sorry we didn't make out" would make Meredith feel like going to another dance with him anytime soon.

Vlad ducked behind his locker door, sneaking occasional peeks at her from behind the gray metal. He took a few deep breaths and closed the door. "Hi, Meredith."

Meredith clutched a folder to her chest and turned toward Vlad. "Hi."

"You have class now, huh?" Oh. My. God. What did he just say? Open foot, insert mouth, Vlad. "I mean, math. Right? You have math?"

Meredith raised a quizzical eyebrow at him. "I have English. Why?"

Vlad's mouth went completely dry with the realization that they shared a class together. He swallowed hard, but apparently, every drop of spit in his body had evaporated. "Just . . . 'cuz."

Vlad thought of crawling into his locker to hide, but he wasn't sure he'd fit. Meredith parted her pretty pink lips, but before she could prolong their already awkward conversation, the locker next to hers closed, revealing a very blonde, much-older-looking-than-last-year Melissa Hart. Meredith and Melissa started talking and soon passed by Vlad and Henry without so much as a glance . . . even when Henry whispered a breathy, "Hi, Melissa."

Henry looked like he might melt into the floor with happiness. After she'd passed, he nudged Vlad and wiggled his eyebrows. "Somebody's been drinking their milk over the summer."

Joss rolled his eyes.

Vlad watched after Meredith, wondering what he'd just said to her, exactly—and what it was about pretty girls that could make a person ramble on like an idiot. After chewing his bottom lip for a moment in contemplation, Vlad closed his locker. "Hey, Joss, Henry's ditching me this afternoon for a student council meeting. You wanna hang out at my house later?"

Joss smiled. "Anything to escape Aunt Matilda's quilting club."

As the trio walked into class, the bell rang shrilly. Mrs. Bell looked up from her book. Vlad had expected crooked teeth, blue hair, and painted-on eyebrows. Instead, he was greeted with straight teeth, tawny brown hair, and painted-on eyebrows. Some things never changed. "Take your seats."

Vlad moved to the back of the room and sat. Henry chose the desk next to his. Joss sat in front of Henry.

Mrs. Bell stood, snapping her book closed. "The bell signifying that class and the school day have begun rings precisely at eight o'clock and I expect you to be in your seats at that time. Not a minute after, not three minutes after. Eight o'clock. I will forgive today with a warning, but the next time we have stragglers"—she flashed a sharp look at Vlad, Henry, and Joss—"detention slips will be handed out."

Vlad looked at Henry and nearly laughed but managed to contain his amusement. Henry was sitting absurdly straight in his seat, with his hands folded neatly on the desk, batting his eyelashes in the direction of Mrs. Bell. Joss glanced back at Henry and smirked.

Mrs. Bell didn't seem to notice. Instead she turned to the chalkboard and began scribbling things that Vlad wasn't paying attention to. He was too busy watching Meredith walk in the door without Mrs. Bell noticing. Meredith scanned the class, offered Vlad a polite nod, and took a seat at the front.

Despite feeling enormously happy to see her, Vlad slid down in his seat.

He wasn't exactly sure why he was avoiding Meredith. It's not like they'd declared their undying love for each other or something stupid like that. It was just a date. Followed by an almost-but-then-not kiss. But ever since then, he'd felt a huge weight on his shoulders. Guilt. He was almost sure of it.

Henry was writing something down in his open notebook. At first Vlad thought it was a note, perhaps some snide comment on Mrs. Bell—or maybe some crucial info on Meredith. But then he realized that everyone was writing . . . everyone but him.

Mrs. Bell snarled. Well, she might not have snarled, but with the expression on her face it was hard to tell. She may have been smiling, but Vlad doubted it very much. People like Mrs. Bell don't smile. They gnash their teeth at innocent passersby. "Vladimir Tod, I suggest you pay attention and get busy copying down this week's assignments."

Thankfully, the rest of first period English flew by, but by the time the bell rang, Vlad was convinced that it was going to be an awful year.

He, Henry, and Joss parted ways for second and third hour, with brief breaks at their lockers that were filled with short conversations about how much biology sucked and how fine arts was okay, that Mr. Kareb was pretty cool for a history teacher and that Mrs. Bell was going to make this the longest school year ever.

After third period, they rushed to the lunchroom and looked around for Greg. They found him sitting with several other popular juniors at the back. After Henry and Joss grabbed trays of hot lunch, Vlad followed them to Greg's table with bagged lunch in hand, where Greg introduced them to his friends.

"Hey, guys, this is my brother, Henry, and my cousin, Joss. And this is Vlad. They're off limits. The only one who gets to shove them inside lockers is me." Greg punched Henry playfully in the arm and smiled at Vlad. "How's the first day going?"

Vlad shrugged. "Okay, I guess."

Vlad had always envied Henry for having such a wonderful family. Henry's parents were thoughtful and generous—even if they did annoy Henry from time to time. Matilda, Henry's mother, baked cookies and other sweet treats every time she knew Vlad was coming over. His father, Peter, had made it a regular habit when he was handing Greg and Henry their allowances to slip Vlad some cash as well. And Greg was tons of fun to hang out with. Vlad couldn't imagine why Henry chose his and Nelly's house to escape to, with all those cool people around. Still, Vlad could stay at Henry's only so often, as being near Henry's parents reminded him how much he missed his own.

One of the boys across the table snatched Vlad's cupcake. Before Vlad could say Stop! the boy took a bite and the blood capsules inside must have burst into his mouth because he turned green. Vlad looked quickly to Henry, whose jaw had hit the table. No one but Henry and Nelly knew Vlad's secret, and now a high schooler had discovered how Vlad had been sneaking blood into the school for nourishment. Vlad looked back at the boy, whose eyes had grown very wide. It looked like he was going to scream.

But instead, he threw up.

Vlad and Henry locked eyes again and then Greg said, "Point of order, gentlemen. Don't take food from Vlad. His aunt can't cook."

The table erupted in laughter.

Vlad breathed a sigh of relief, and after the group moved to a new table, he finished his blood-mixed-with-strawberry-jam sandwich quietly.

After lunch and three more hours of first-day notes, new people, getting lost, and noticing that Meredith shared only one of his classes, but Henry was in three, and Joss was in five, Vlad arrived at his locker at the end of the day triumphant, but exhausted. He'd survived the first day of his freshman year virtually unscathed.

He pulled his backpack out of his locker and glanced down the hall for any sign of Henry. Unfortunately, leather-clad shoulders obstructed his view.

Bill turned and, despite Vlad's effort to shrink inside his locker, saw Vlad. He tapped Tom on the shoulder, and they locked on to Vlad with their menacing eyes. They both wore leather jackets—probably an attempt to appear tough to any of the older bullies who might try anything with the two hotheaded freshmen. To Vlad's dismay, they sauntered closer. Bill slammed Vlad's locker shut. Vlad watched as the strap of his backpack got caught in the locker door, like a snake that had wormed its way through an incredibly tight space and then gotten stuck. Vlad looked from Bill to Tom, who was cracking his knuckles loudly. "Hey, goth boy. We didn't get to finish our little chat earlier."

He was dead. After his luck at getting away this morning, after having survived almost his entire first day of his freshman year, Vlad was going to die. He could picture his tombstone now: HERE LIES VLADIMIR TOD, BEATEN TO DEATH BY THE TWO MISSING LINKS.

"Hey, Vlad. What's going on?" Joss leaned against the locker next to his and raised his eyebrows.

Vlad glanced at Joss. What was this guy, a trained bodyguard? Some kind of heroic stalker? Not that it was a bad thing to know that someone had your back, but still . . . it was mildly embarrassing to know that he had to be rescued, like some loser in distress.

He wanted to tell Joss to run, to get out of there while he still could, because Vlad was about to get the beating of his life, and anyone who associated with Vlad might be subject to the same punishment. But instead, he shoved Bill out of the way and opened his locker again. "Lay off, caveman."

To Vlad's horror, Joss gave Bill's shoulder a light push, almost like they were ganging up on the bullies together. "You're not giving Vlad any trouble, are you? Not after our little talk this morning."

"Freshman, he's about to enter the kidney donor program. If you don't wanna join him, I suggest you back off."

Vlad wrinkled his forehead. How would that work, exactly? If the idea was to punch a kidney out, he was pretty sure it wouldn't be a viable organ anymore. And what was with Bill calling Joss "freshman"? He and Tom were in the same grade as Vlad and Joss.

Bill swiveled around until he was facing Vlad again and raised his fist. Vlad got ready to dodge, but in a blink, Joss had Bill by the wrist and flipped him around, pinning his fist behind him. Joss shoved Bill into the locker until Bill's cheek was perfectly flat against the metal. "Now, I want you to listen really closely to what I'm about to tell you. Leave Vlad alone. Or next time, I'll break your arm. You got me?"

He released Bill just as Mrs. Bell rounded the corner. She flashed them all a disapproving snarl, but Vlad didn't think she'd seen Joss's karate-fast reflexes.

Tom grabbed Bill by the sleeve, and they moved quickly down the hall and out the front doors without another word.

Again. Just like this morning. Once more, Vlad had been a loser in distress, despite shoving Bill back. Once more, someone else had come to his aid, because Vlad hadn't been capable of defending himself.

His thoughts trailed briefly to Otis's letter and the notion of mind control.

He grabbed his backpack and shut the locker door. "Thanks. I owe you one."

Joss shrugged, as if it had been no big deal. "So you said earlier we could hang out. I just got *Race to Armageddon* for the PS2 and—"

Vlad held up a hand, his initial irritation at being rescued quickly melting away. "Dude, I've got *Race to Armageddon 2*."

"What's the difference?"

Vlad shook his head. "What rock does your family live under?" He moved down the hall toward the exit, gesturing for Joss to follow.

Three hours later they were sprawled in front of the couch in Vlad's living room, surrounded by potato chip bags and empty Pepsi cans. Joss's eyes were wide with amazement. "That's the goriest game I've ever seen."

Vlad smiled. It felt good to hang out with someone besides Henry. Henry, of course, was his closest friend in the world. But Joss was pretty cool. Besides, Joss was just a regular guy—probably as imperfect as Vlad. Henry was great, but Vlad got tired of always being in his shadow.

That, and it was nice to actually win a video game once in a while.

Nelly poked her head out of the kitchen. "Vladimir, is your new friend staying for dinner?"

Vlad looked at Joss, who blushed and nodded. "I'll have to call Aunt Matilda, but yeah . . . I'd love to."

Nelly handed Joss the phone, and he stepped into the other room.

Once Vlad could hear mumbled conversation, he turned to Nelly. "Let me guess . . . spaghetti again?"

Nelly just smiled.

Spaghetti was the easiest food that they'd found to hide blood in whenever company was over. That is, company that wasn't Henry. Vlad hated the slimy noodles, but blood mixed with tomato sauce—and just a hint of oregano—was pretty tasty, so he didn't mind that much.

Joss came back to the living room, looking happy and relieved. "She said I can stay, but I have to go home right after."

Knowing it would be a while before dinner was ready, Vlad led Joss upstairs, pausing on the steps to scratch Amenti behind the ears. As they passed through the library, Joss gasped. "Wow, you have a great collection of books."

Vlad raised a curious brow. He didn't know many guys his age that were much into reading. With a smile, he pointed to the set of shelves nearest his bedroom door. "Those are my favorites over there."

Joss ran his fingers over the spines of the books. *The Practice and Theory of Telepathy, Vlad Tepes: A History,*

Myths and Legends of Our Modern World, Vampires: Real or Make-Believe? He paused with his fingertips on the vampire book and glanced over his shoulder at Vlad. "So what do you think? Are vampires real or just some pretend nightmare that people keep writing about?"

At first, Vlad said nothing. Then, after Joss looked over his collection for several minutes, it became clear that he was really expecting Vlad to answer. Given how many years Vlad had been pretending to be human, his reply came as second nature. "Nobody believes in vampires, but that book does present some pretty good arguments."

His tone turned serious as he met Joss's eyes. "Personally, I think that anything is possible."

Joss nodded.

Vlad opened his bedroom door and gave a quick glance around before inviting Joss in. His room was cluttered with dirty laundry, but Vlad tossed the clothes behind the door and sat on the bed. "So where'd you move from anyway?"

Joss was looking about the room, curiously approving what he saw with a nod. "Santa Carla. Before that, I lived in Romania, and before that, New Orleans, Paris, and San Francisco."

"You move around a lot."

A sad glimmer lurked in Joss's eyes. "It's my dad's job. I hate it. It'd be nice to stay in one place for a while."

Joss shook his head and managed a smile. "Hey, have you ever seen what happens when you drop Mentos in diet soda?"

Vlad smiled. At least things would be more interesting with Joss around.

4

Psycho Slasher Chain-saw Guy from Hell

WHAT ABOUT *HER*?"

Vlad sighed. They were never going to go to the movies if Henry didn't stop asking what every girl who passed was thinking. It wouldn't normally bother Vlad—he was totally curious, himself, and for the last two hours solid, he'd been both willing and able to traipse through the minds of cute girls—but the fact that he might be missing out on the filmtastic gore and mayhem of *Psycho Slasher Chain-saw Guy from Hell* was starting to make his eye twitch. He'd been waiting six weeks, ever since the first day of school, to see this film. Waiting even one more minute might make his brain explode.

He turned his twitching eyes to the long-legged blonde standing outside the theater. Her tiny feet were wedged into high heels, and her long, muscular legs reached all the way up to the small strip of cotton that passed for a skirt. He took a deep breath and focused on her. Ever so gently, he pushed with his mind.

She frowned. These heels were killing her feet, but whatever. Just as long as she looked nice for Brad. And so help her, if that snob Brenda Carlton took her seat by Brad one more time, it was hair-pulling time. Where was Brad, anyway? Oooh, there's a cute boy. Henry something. What's his name? He goes to Bathory, has an older brother. McMillan! God, he's hot. But what's with the scrawny, pale kid next to him? Word to the wise, honey, get a tan . . . and a gym membership.

Vlad pulled out of her mind with a snort. He glanced over at Henry, who was wearing an expectant look on his face. "So? What's she thinking?"

Vlad watched the girl and nodded. "She thinks I'm hot."

Henry's eyes followed. "Nice."

Vlad looked up at the clock on the wall. "Movie starts in ten minutes. We better get in line."

Henry's eyes were locked on a short, curvy brunette who was walking out of a lingerie shop. "One more."

Vlad groaned. "Okay, but that's it. I need some bloodshed after this."

Henry chuckled. "It'll make you hungry. Seeing a gory movie always does. And my mom won't pick us up for another two hours. Have you considered that?"

"Don't care. I've been dying to see this for weeks. So let's go already."

"One more and we'll go. I swear." Henry nodded toward the brunette, who'd stopped to rifle through her purse. "Besides, Otis said to practice your telepathy. I'm helping."

With an impatient sigh, Vlad looked at the young woman and mentally pushed with a dizzying rush of blood to the head.

Where on earth were her keys? If she didn't hurry, she was going to be late for her waxing appointment across town. Let's see, she bought a new blouse, new shoes, new bra. All she needed now was to pick up some tampo—

Vlad pulled out of her mind as fast as he could. He dropped his gaze to the floor and tugged Henry toward the Stokerton mall movie theater.

Henry looked from Vlad to the girl and back. "What is it? What was she thinking?"

Vlad shivered, trying to block out the girl's last thought from his mind. "Trust me. You don't want to know."

"Henry!" A familiar squeal echoed down the hall from near the food court. Stephanie Brawn, her sister (whatever her name was . . . Vlad was beginning to think her name might just be "Stephanie's sister"), Carrie Anderson, and a group of fairly popular kids were standing in a group. The girls waved to Henry, sending a bolt of nausea through Vlad's stomach. Several of the guys nodded to him. Vlad shifted his weight from one foot to the other. What did they expect? It wasn't like his best friend was going to ditch him just like that. Not after plotting and planning to come see the goriest movie ever made, not after spending the entire day reading girls' minds, not after—

Henry slapped him on the shoulder. "Be right back, Vlad."

And before Vlad could let out a troubled "dude!" Henry was swept away by his ever-growing popularity, and Vlad was left standing with his jaw on the floor. Almost immediately, he snapped his mouth shut and slid his thumbs in his front pockets, glancing around in an effort to appear cool and casual. He wasn't sure if it was working, but he was sure of one thing: Henry was totally treating him to junk food . . . if they ever managed to actually enter the theater.

Across the hall, a pale, skinny kid handed a flyer to a passing goth kid, who Vlad recognized as one of the goths he'd seen hanging out on the steps at Bathory High. Vlad almost waved but then realized how stupid that would be. He didn't actually know the guy; he'd only just watched him from his secret sanctuary in the bell tower. The two chatted about some new club for a minute, and then the goth who Vlad knew but didn't know walked into theater five.

At least *somebody* was going to see *Psycho Slasher Chainsaw Guy from Hell.*

Vlad glanced back at Henry, who looked to be sharing a secret with Stephanie's sister. The looks the other popular kids were giving Henry were shining and full of approval—it was so annoying. But that was Henry. Good-looking, smart, great grades, life of the party, tan, and perfect in every way. Vlad chewed his bottom lip thoughtfully and with a glimpse at the clock, groaned. They were going to miss it, the best movie of all time. All because Henry had to hang out with kids who'd never really be his friends.

Vlad watched Henry talk to the girl and flexed his mind. Not a lot. Just a little. Then suddenly, he was silently floating among Henry's thoughts.

Henry finished whispering that he'd loved tasting her strawberry lip gloss yesterday after school and pulled away. He was sure to wink at Stephanie, who was turning red from jealousy over him flirting with her little sister. Henry had no idea what her name was . . . just that she was pretty easy when it came to kissing, and that she didn't talk much, which, if you think about it, must be pretty difficult to do when you're making out all the time.

Vlad rolled his eyes. Didn't Henry think about anything but girls? He took a deep breath and focused, just like Otis's instructions had said.

Henry raised a single finger to his nose, and then flicked a booger across the hall.

The girls jumped back in disgust. The boys laughed but mumbled a collective, "We've gotta go." Henry was left standing there with his forehead creased, wondering just why he'd picked his nose like that in front of his friends.

Henry flashed a glance at Vlad. His shock melted into a look of horrified understanding.

Vlad's smirk quickly faded.

"Henry . . ."

Henry moved past him, toward the theater. "Don't. Just don't."

Weighed down by guilt, Vlad slowly followed.

Then Vlad smirked. Maybe next time Henry ditched him, he'd make him dance the macarena.

After spending the last of their cash on two tickets, an extra-large popcorn, Milk Duds, Sour Skittles, chocolate-covered raisins, gummy worms, and two "Giganto" sodas, Vlad and Henry gathered up their feast and headed into number nine, where the goriest movie ever was about to begin. The theater was incredibly dark, and on the way up the stairs, Vlad almost lost sight of Henry, but then he heard the crunch of popcorn under his feet ahead of him and figured he'd do the Hansel and Gretel thing. After a moment, his eyes adjusted, and he focused on a pair of long, shapely, miniskirt-wearing legs that were climbing the stairs in front of him. On the back of the woman's knee Vlad could just barely make out a thick blue vein. When she took a step, it pulsed slightly. Vlad's fangs shot from his gums. He clamped his mouth shut and forced his attention away from the woman's delectable-looking veins. He stared at the floor, the other moviegoers, anything that wasn't sending waves of dire hunger through his stomach. Once he reached the seat beside Henry, his thirst had calmed some.

The previews were starting. Vlad reached for the Milk Duds and chuckled at Henry, whose face was hovering just inches from the top of the popcorn bucket. His eyes were locked on the screen, and he was shoveling popcorn into his mouth until his cheeks resembled that of a squirrel stocking up for winter.

On the screen, a young guy with long hair ran through the woods with a panicked scream. There was a moment of silence and then a loud shriek, followed shortly by an enormous amount of blood splashing against the camera. Henry gasped. Vlad's stomach rumbled.

Two hours later, the boys walked out of the movie theater with gaping mouths. Henry dropped the empty popcorn tub in the trash. "That was awesome! For once, the ads were right—that *was* the goriest film ever made."

Vlad took one last sip of soda and sat the empty cup on top of the overflowing trash can. "Just remember that if Nelly asks, we saw *SpyGuy 009: Die Again Tomorrow Forever.*"

Henry's brother, Greg, was standing just outside the movie theater door, wearing a smirk. "About time. I thought *SpyGuy 009* got out over a half hour ago."

Vlad beamed. "It did. We saw *Psycho Slasher Chain-saw Guy from Hell.*"

Greg nodded approvingly. "I saw that last Friday. That scene with the hedge clippers? Brutal."

"I thought Mom was picking us up."

Greg shrugged. "You thought wrong."

The three of them made a large loop away from the hedge near the wall and walked toward Greg's car. Vlad glanced over his shoulder at the hedge, still picturing the gory movie scene involving hedge clippers, and shuddered.

He couldn't imagine what it would be like to be hunted down and gutted. Hunted down, yes. But gutted? The thought gave Vlad a shiver.

5
KILLER AT LARGE

THE VAMPIRE SLAYER flipped open the latches on the old wooden case and ran his fingers over the soft velvet lining inside. One by one, he removed his tools and laid them gently on the cotton cloth he'd spread on the floor for inspection. It was nearly time to begin his hunt. He had to be sure he was prepared.

He hefted the weight of the silver crucifix in his hand before laying it down on the cloth. He followed it with three bottles of serum, the rosary, the small hatchet that had been a gift from his grandfather, and the wooden stake—a beautiful instrument carved from ash and tipped in pure silver. He wondered, yet again, how many of the undead his great-great-uncle had taken down with this same stake. The slayer always thought about him whenever he opened the case. After all, the vampire killing kit had been invented by his great-great-uncle, Professor Ernst Blomberg, and passed down through the family since the mid-1800s. It was a long-standing tradition, as was keeping your slayer trade secret from everyone in the family other than those who had slain before you and those who would slay after you. There were over a hundred slayer families, of course, but only one slayer per generation ever joined the Slayer Society. And only a slayer could recognize the traits of the next slayer in his family line.

Thinking back to the day he learned he was next in line, the slayer realized that he should have been pleased to be part of an ancient and honored tradition. But neither honor, nor notoriety in the Society's close-knit circle, had convinced him to surrender to fate—it had been Cecile. Dear, pretty Cecile, with her blonde curls framing her tiny, freckled face, and her large green eyes, which had sparkled like emeralds.

It had been an unusually dark, quiet night, and the lack of the usual household noises had woken him. From down the hall, he heard a tiny whimper. Cecile—his darling baby sister, probably having a nightmare. As any good sibling would, he crept down the hall to check on her, but what he found still haunted him to this day. It was what had driven him to accept his post as a vampire slayer. It was what pushed him on, every moment of every day, to hunt down the beasts and take their lives.

He had turned the doorknob slowly, and the door swung open. Looming over a pale, unconscious Cecile was a vampire—her blood dripping from it fangs. After that, his memories were a blur. But he remembered clearly that it had been the day of her funeral that he'd been sworn in as a slayer, and just before the final blow in every battle with a vampire, he'd uttered the words, "For you, Cecile."

He looked over his tools. They were all in fine order. Apart from being a little low on holy water, the slayer was ready. He turned the stake over in his hands and smirked at a passing memory of an old film, in which a slayer was portrayed as a bumbling fool with a sack full of splintered wood. How ridiculous. A true slayer needed only one stake to take a blood drinker down. One stake and good aim. The heart is a small organ and, what's more, hidden behind the ribs. If you don't hit it just right, you're going to have a very angry vampire on your hands. And nobody wants that.

He remembered one of his first slayings with a sigh. It had gone well. He'd staked the vampire. No fuss, no muss. But after he turned to collect his tools he heard a noise. Whistling. He turned back to the undead monster. The whistling got louder. Something was wrong.

The vampire sat up.

Apparently, he'd missed the heart and punctured a lung. It was a rookie mistake, the first and only time he'd missed the heart. Lesson learned. A punctured lung was enough to slow down an older vampire but not enough to kill it. The more the vampire exerted itself to stand, the louder it whistled. It was like doing battle with the little engine that wants to drink your blood. He staked the monster again and had burned the body, just to be safe.

He slipped the stake back into its spot in the walnut case and moved on to the other tools, wiping each off with the corner of the cloth before returning it home. These tools were his partners, his compatriots. He'd carried this case with him since he was ten years old and would one day pass it on to another member of his family—perhaps a nephew, a niece, or even one of his own children. There was no telling. Only a slayer could identify another slayer, and he had not yet seen another in his bloodline younger than himself.

He pinched the bridge of his nose and squeezed his eyes shut, suppressing a yawn. Outside, the sun was just peeking over the horizon. There was time for rest, and then, after another quick review of the small town of Bathory, he would begin his hunt for the vampire he'd been hired to kill.

6

HALLOWEEN

VLAD PULLED THE black hood over his head and regarded his reflection in the mirror. The only costume that could top last year's was going as the one thing everyone—both humans and vampires—were afraid of.

Death.

Glancing at the clock, he took a moment to reread Otis's latest letter.

> *Dearest Vladimir,*
>
> *My apologies. This letter will be brief, as I am wait-ing to board a plane to Paris as I write this. I will send a longer letter soon, but for now my time is stretched.*

I was disappointed to hear that you have had only minimal success in manipulating people's thought processes, but I cannot help but question whether or not you are really putting forth an effort to control them, Vlad. I understand the difficulties that come with attempting to control someone close to you, but strangers should be fairly easy to control. Please continue to practice, and I will see what assistance I can find on this matter.

Please tell Nelly that her last letter was greatly appreciated, and that I am saddened that I have no time to respond at present, but that I will soon. I promise.

Be well.

Yours in Eternity,

Otis

Vlad grabbed his plastic sickle and headed downstairs, where Nelly was filling a large plastic cauldron with gummy eyeballs and flavored wax fangs. Vlad looked into the cauldron and groaned. "Do you have to give out all the fangs? Can't you save some for me?"

Nelly chuckled and dropped another handful of candy in the cauldron. "You have enough fangs."

The doorbell rang and Vlad opened it to Henry, who was dressed as a zombie—complete with missing arm and rotting skin—and Joss, who was wearing slacks, a button-down shirt, and an unbuttoned vest. Vlad raised an eyebrow. "Joss, I thought you were dressing up."

Henry smacked Joss on the back of the head. "I told you! Go on, tell him what you're supposed to be."

Joss's eyes grew wide at Henry's disgust, and he spoke as if it were the most obvious thing in the world. "I'm an anthropologist."

Vlad looked at Henry, who rolled his eyes. "Dude, can't you tell people that you're a serial killer or something? How am I gonna get Melissa to dance with me if my cousin's an anthropologist?"

Joss shrugged. "Maybe she'll think anthropologists are hot."

Nelly chimed in with that parental tone that she used whenever she meant business. "I assume that there's no big surprise at midnight this year."

Vlad wrinkled his brow. "No. Why?"

Nelly smiled. "Good. Home by eleven, Vladimir."

Vlad rolled his eyes, but he didn't dare question Nelly. Instead, he led Henry and Joss out the front door and down the street. They were halfway to Matthew's house when Vlad noticed a trio of nervous trick-or-treaters rushing to the other side of the street. After a moment of curious con-fusion, he recognized the one in the middle and felt a rush of guilt at having scared the kid last year, all for want of impressing Henry and the promise of sticky sweet treats.

Henry nudged Vlad with his elbow. "You okay?"

Vlad adjusted the hood over his head and shrugged. "Yeah, fine."

At the end of the street, cars were pausing in front of an excessively decorated house. It looked like Matthew's mom had gone all out this year. Standing on the porch was a group of girls. At the center stood a sparkly red devil, complete with glitter-covered horns. Meredith brushed her hair from her face with one of the tines of her plastic pitchfork. Vlad felt his heart punch his insides, as if it might tear free at any moment. He placed his hand against his chest, just in case.

Henry smirked. "Meredith looks pretty tonight."

Meredith did look pretty. Breathtaking, in fact. But that didn't mean Vlad was any closer to having any clue what to say to her.

Unfortunately, Joss had also noticed how great Meredith looked. "Wow . . ."

Both Vlad and Henry shot Joss a warning look, but he either ignored them or didn't notice, because he moved forward and stepped up onto the porch. He was smiling at Meredith, who in turn smiled at Henry, when Henry grabbed Joss by the sleeve and pulled him into the house. Vlad ducked behind them and went inside as well.

Maybe next year he'd save them all a lot of trouble and come as the invisible man.

Matthew's parents had set up most of the party in their newly refurbished basement—a large room with two couches, a pool table, and a dartboard. His father had plugged in some DJ equipment and, thankfully, was playing what must have been music from Matthew's CD collection when the boys made their way downstairs.

Black and orange streamers draped overhead in long, twisted lines. Black and orange balloons were floating everywhere and bumping against the ceiling with every thump of bass. A few kids were dancing, but most were hovering around the punch bowl and laughing. Every few seconds, someone would wave frantically and shout Henry's name. Vlad wondered how long it would take for Henry to abandon him, but to Henry's credit, he stuck fairly close to Vlad and Joss for the next hour.

Unfortunately, popularity is a lot like gravity. There's no use fighting it. So Vlad understood when Henry mumbled that he'd be right back, which was code for *I'll see you after the party*, and disappeared into the growing crowd. It didn't take long before Joss disappeared into the crowd as well, leaving Vlad alone in a room full of about thirty people.

It was hard sometimes, trying to discern whether Henry had continued to be his friend over the years despite their differences because Henry really liked him, or because Henry felt a weird bound-by-blood, his-duty-as-a-drudge connection to him. Vlad didn't like to think about it much. Because if

Henry wasn't his real friend, if all the stuff they'd gone through was nothing but some vampire-controlling hoax, then he really didn't want to know.

Still . . . it did make him wonder sometimes.

Vlad finished his punch, wishing the red liquid were more than just syrupy, sugary water, and navigated his way through the crowd until he was upstairs and outside, in the cool quiet of evening. All of the laughter, talking, and noise was going to give him a headache if he didn't take in the revelry in small doses. He stepped off the porch and walked around the side of the house.

A gawky, skinny boy with an old 35 mm camera hanging around his neck was sitting on a picnic table bench in the backyard. Vlad considered ducking back around the front of the house, but the boy looked positively miserable, and Vlad knew what it felt like when you were struggling to fit in. He moved closer and managed a smile. "Hey, Eddie."

Eddie barely lifted his head to glance at Vlad. His voice was soft and hushed. "Hi, Vlad."

If there were a more unpopular kid in the town of Bathory than Vladimir Tod, it was Eddie Poe. Eddie's parents were pretty well off as far as money went, but still they insisted on buying Eddie's clothes from the thrift store and couldn't, it seemed, pay enough attention to their son to see he should be wearing clothes two sizes bigger than what they were buying. Eddie's glasses had been cracked for as long as Vlad could recall, and he was constantly cradling what was obviously his most cherished possession, his camera. Vlad nodded to it. "Get any good pictures of the party?"

Eddie shrugged. "I haven't gone inside yet. My mom made me come. I wanted to stay home."

Vlad nodded sympathetically. He could see why Eddie hadn't wanted to come. It was tough attempting to be social with people who'd rather pretend you didn't exist—especially when it was a Halloween party and your parents wouldn't even spring for a costume. Vlad slid the robe over his head and laid his plastic sickle on the table. "Man, this thing is hot." He raised an eyebrow at Eddie. "Hey, you wouldn't want to wear it for a while, would ya? Maybe keeping an eye on my sickle for me?"

A spark lit up in Eddie's eyes, but it was quickly followed by suspicion. "I guess. But . . . why are you being nice to me?"

Vlad smiled. Eddie's suspicious reaction had been expected. After all, almost everyone at school picked on Eddie, so he'd been conditioned to expect that every act of kindness was a mean trick in disguise. "Nice to you? You'd be doing me a favor. I might melt in that thing."

Vlad swore he could see tears lurking in Eddie's eyes as Eddie slipped the robe on. Eddie picked up the sickle and strode bravely toward the house. He paused and looked back at Vlad. "Thanks."

Vlad scratched his wrist and shrugged, still smiling, and sat on the bench. "No problem."

He waited for Eddie to leave, but Eddie's feet seemed frozen to the spot. His eyes were locked on Vlad's.

Vlad raised an eyebrow. "Eddie? Something wrong?"

But judging by the horrified look in Eddie's eyes, Vlad didn't need to ask. Something was wrong. *Very* wrong, judging by the way Eddie's chest was rising and falling in startled breaths.

Vlad was about to ask what, when Eddie whispered aloud the three words that had haunted Vlad's dreams for many years. "W-what are you?"

Vlad shrugged and tried hard to keep his tone even, despite the fact that he was completely freaking out on the inside. He ran the tip of his tongue over his teeth. Nothing. His fangs hadn't betrayed him. It was somewhat comforting, but not enough to calm the racing of his heart. "What are you talking about?"

Eddie glanced over his shoulder at the house, as if judging the small distance between him and safety. "Y-you're n-not human. Are you?"

Vlad forced a laugh, but it didn't even sound convincing to him. "Not human? Man, Eddie, what did they put in that punch?"

Eddie gripped his camera tightly, but, Vlad noticed, he didn't run. "You're some kind of monster, aren't you? My mom, she says monsters aren't real. But I saw one last year, and now . . . now I'm seeing another one, aren't I?"

Inside Vlad's chest, his heart was slamming against his ribs. The flight half of his fight-or-flight response was on the verge of winning out but hadn't quite yet. Vlad kept his cool. "I don't know what you're talking about."

"Your eyes. They turned purple for a minute. That's not normal, not human." Eddie took a shuddering breath and released it. "So what are you?"

Oh no.

How did his eyes flash without being triggered? Vlad glanced down at his wrist and briefly recalled scratching it with his other hand. Great. Now he was going to have to worry about touching his own tattoo, too? Touching his mark, his name in Elysian code, had never triggered the weird purple-eye response before, and hadn't ever since the day Otis drank his blood and infused Vlad with his essence, burning the tattoo into Vlad's tender flesh. Why would it start now?

"I'll tell you what I am, Eddie. I'm not amused. You should be careful what kind of things you accuse people of." Vlad met his eyes, hoping his sincerity would be enough to convince Eddie.

Eddie's eyes grew wide with fear once again. "Why? What are you gonna do to me?"

"Nothing, Eddie." Vlad shook his head. His heart had tired of raging against his insides and had settled into his stomach in defeat. "Look, I think you need to talk to your mom about canceling the sci-fi channel. I'm just a kid, like you. Now leave me alone, okay?"

A full, silver moon hung above, and when Vlad lay back on the bench, it was perfectly framed by a thousand shimmering stars. He listened to Eddie's footsteps as they retreated inside and sighed in relief. Music drifted out from the house, but it was soft enough at this distance for Vlad to ignore it. He shut out his thoughts, not wanting to really think about anything but the moon and stars. A cool breeze brushed his cheeks, and Vlad closed his eyes.

What was he going to do about Eddie? He couldn't tell Nelly or Otis—they worried enough as it was. All he could hope for was that Eddie would wake up tomorrow and realize that his eyes had played tricks on him on the spookiest night of the year. After all, it was pretty easy to get freaked out on Halloween, what with all the stories going around this time of year about werewolves, ghosts, and vampires.

Vlad swallowed nervously.

"Well, well, well. Look what we have here, Tom." At Bill's first word, Vlad opened his eyes and sat up, but Bill shoved him back down on the bench with an open, heavy hand.

Above him, quickly blocking his view of the moon, was Bill's bulbous head, grinning with an evil glint in his eye.

Joining him after a second was a sinister-looking Tom. "You're gonna get it now, goth boy."

Before Vlad could blink, Bill yanked him off the bench and held him aloft. Vlad struggled and tried to kick free. A strangled, "Let me go, dorkwad" managed to escape his throat amid a myriad of curses. Bill shook him, and he glanced at the house, wondering how likely it would be they'd get interrupted by one of Matthew's parents. But inside, the party raged on, and no one seemed to notice that Vlad was in trouble. Serious trouble.

Before Vlad knew what was coming, he felt the meaty thud of Bill's fist against his jaw.

It didn't hurt. Not really. But Vlad's face grew very warm and his jaw tingled with something that might have been pain if it hadn't been for his rising temper. Wriggling out of Bill's grip, Vlad dropped to the ground and tried to stand, but Tom stepped closer and punched him hard in the stomach.

That hurt.

And for a moment, Vlad couldn't breathe.

When the air finally returned to his lungs, he coughed hard and struggled to stand. He'd almost made it to his feet when Bill slugged him in the eye. Behind him—or somewhere, Vlad couldn't be sure where exactly—Tom said, "That's what you get, goth boy! That's what you get!"

Vlad cupped his hand over his eye. Inside his mouth, his fangs sprang from his gums, slicing into his already bleeding tongue. Vlad's stomach rumbled. His throat felt dry, parched with an almost uncontrollable thirst. He kept his mouth closed and glared with his uncovered eye at his attackers. He was pretty sure he could duck by Tom and make it to the sidewalk, but what then? Those jerks punched each other for fun and could run faster than you'd think two refrigerators could move. He needed a plan. And he needed it fast.

His eye pulsed against his palm. His heart was hammering so hard against the inside of his chest that it seemed one long, continuous beat. He took a step to the left, and Bill and Tom followed suit. Vlad pursed his lips. He had to fight to keep his fangs hidden. "What's your problem?"

Several kids from the party had found their way outside and were watching the scene with intrigue. A few shouted encouragement, egging on the fight, but most watched in stunned silence. No one called for an adult or stepped forward to help Vlad. And where were Henry and Joss?

Tom took a step closer, and Vlad resisted moving backward. "You are."

Hands closed over Vlad's shoulders and pushed. Bill and Tom proceeded to shove Vlad back and forth like a human Ping-Pong ball. Well, half-human, anyway. Vlad pulled away and made a break for the crowd, but Bill yanked him back by the collar and threw him to the ground. Tom stomped hard on the center of Vlad's chest, and the memory of what it had felt like when D'Ablo broke one of his ribs pierced his imagination. Vlad kicked and tried to wriggle free, but Bill's foot had him pinned. Tom grinned over him and raised his foot over Vlad's face.

In a flash, Vlad was up. He shoved Tom as hard as he could and bolted for the edge of the crowd.

Tom hit the ground several yards away with a thud and swore loudly.

Vlad turned his head to where Tom was lying and raised an eyebrow, astounded at how Tom had flown so far with just a shove.

Henry broke through the crowd and flashed a surprised glimpse at Tom before directing his attention to Vlad. His lips remained silent, but his eyes asked if Vlad was okay. Vlad nodded and brushed the grass from his jeans.

Matthew's mom burst out the back door and, though it was a case of too little, too late, said, "What on earth is going on out here?"

Bill helped Tom up and they hurried down the street, with Tom cradling his right arm in his left.

Vlad watched after them. A slight smirk touched his lips.

Henry tugged on his sleeve, and they tried to slink back into the house unseen, but it was too late. Matthew's mom had spotted Vlad's bruised, puffy face. She brought them inside, wrapped some ice in a kitchen towel, and handed it to Vlad. Then, to Vlad's horror, she picked up the phone. "Hi, Nelly. This is Karen, Matthew's mom?"

Henry sat beside Vlad on the couch and muttered, "What happened?"

Vlad kept his voice low. "They were just being their charming selves. But I handled it."

Henry's eyes got wide, and Vlad didn't have to read his mind to know that he was going to ask how Vlad had managed to knock Tom down like that, but before he could, Mike Brennan sat down on the other side of Vlad. "I've never seen anybody who could knock that guy on his butt—he's a wall," Mike said.

Vlad glanced at Henry, who looked equally confounded. Mike chuckled.

Several people smiled at Vlad—as if suddenly realizing that they were in the presence of greatness. Vlad pulled the ice pack away from his eye and touched the bruises with the tips of his fingers. Other than the pain of being beaten up by two of the biggest jerks known to mankind, it was a pretty good moment. He glanced around the room. Meredith was nowhere to be found.

Neither was Joss.

Vlad turned to Henry, to ask if he'd seen his cousin, when the front door opened and a furious Nelly walked in, still wearing her slippers. Henry shrank into the couch. Vlad wished he could follow suit, but there was no use prolonging the inevitable. He stood and handed his ice pack over to Matthew's mom.

Nelly barked, "Car. Now."

Vlad sighed and, with slumped shoulders, stood and followed Nelly to the car. The doors had barely closed before Nelly raised her voice, causing Vlad to wince with each syllable. "Vladimir, I am so disappointed in you. Fighting? What's next? Biting people?"

Vlad tried to keep his eyes from getting any wider but must have failed miserably, as Nelly's voice went up another octave. "You didn't bite anyone, did you?"

"No." Vlad looked at the door handle with longing, but it was no use. There was no escaping once they got you in the car. "I wouldn't do that, Nelly. You act like I haven't been hiding what I am for the last fourteen years. I'm not some stupid kid. I know better than to bite people—no matter how much they might deserve it."

Nelly seemed to weigh this in her mind for a moment, and then in a much calmer voice said, "I don't want you fighting."

After a moment, she glanced at Vlad, as if expecting a reply. She didn't get one.

Nelly began navigating the car down the street and sighed, the tension in her voice softening some, but not enough to put Vlad at ease. "You *must* be more careful. You could have been hurt. *They* could've been hurt! What if you'd lost control? Right there, in front of all those people."

"I am careful." Vlad kept quiet about Tom's wrist, still unsure how he'd managed to send Tom flying. He settled back in his seat and stared out the window, wishing they were home already and that this whole evening were over.

"I can only imagine how quickly people would reach for torches and pitchforks to try to drive you out of town." Nelly shook her head again as she brought the car to a stop in their driveway. She turned to Vlad and wiped a tear from her cheek.

The pain deep in Vlad's chest was much worse than his eye. Not only had he gotten beat up but he had also just been reminded of what a freak he really was by the one person it was supposed to matter to least.

"What if they tried . . ." Nelly's voice trailed off. "I couldn't bear it. I lost your parents, Vladimir. I can't lose you, too."

Vlad dropped his gaze to the floor. "That's not going to happen, Nelly. It was just a fight. My secret is safe."

Vlad's thoughts turned to Eddie, and a peculiar nausea massaged his insides.

Nelly was quiet for a moment, and then sighed in relief. She opened her door and muttered under her breath in an afterthought, "I have a good mind to ground you."

Vlad raised his eyebrows. He was almost positive Nelly would do no such thing, but he vowed to behave over the next few weeks, just in case. Besides, he felt pretty bad about worrying her so much.

But it was pretty funny watching Bill and Tom run away like a couple of scared babies. And it served them right for picking on someone smaller than them.

Vlad opened his door, and turning his head so that Nelly couldn't see, he cracked a triumphant smile.

7

AN UNEXPECTED INVITATION

MEREDITH STRETCHED HER ARMS over her head and parted her pretty pink lips in a yawn. From the other side of the cafeteria, Vlad sighed and tore his gaze away from her. Across the table from him, Henry and Joss were having their now-usual argument.

"I'm telling you, there's no way Stephanie's sister is a better kisser than Stephanie." Joss shook his head, cracking a grin.

Vlad stole a sip of Henry's chocolate milk and stayed quiet, trying not to think about how he was the only guy in Bathory High who Stephanie and her sister hadn't kissed. Not that he wanted to kiss either of them.

His eyes found Meredith again.

Henry laughed. "I'm telling you, Joss! Stephanie is a great kisser, but her sister . . ."

Vlad shook his head. They'd been comparing notes for two weeks now, ever since Joss made out with Stephanie one day behind the school, rather than going to detention. It was nauseating.

"Okay then, what makes her better, exactly?"

"Tongue." Henry grinned, and even the upperclassmen at the table guffawed, slapping Henry high fives.

Vlad looked over at Meredith. Noticing him, she smiled and raised her fingertips in a small wave, but Vlad felt his cheeks flush and tore his gaze away, staring intently at the table instead. He couldn't think of anyone who could leave him so speechless. He dared a glance back and met her eyes. Then, with a deep breath, lifted his hand off the table and waved.

But he couldn't be certain she saw him do it, because Melissa Hart had sat down next to her, drawing Meredith's attention away again.

The argument about who was a better kisser carried on throughout the last part of the school day, giving Vlad an excuse not to contribute to the conversation. What he really wanted to do was to think about how he might apologize to Meredith, if he were brave enough, and to reflect on Eddie and whether or not he'd changed his mind about Vlad since the Halloween party. Vlad shivered at the thought.

After the last bell rang and Vlad stepped outside, flanked by Henry and Joss, he squinted up into the too-bright sun and adjusted the strap of the heavy backpack on his shoulder. "Today's the day. I'm calling Meredith."

Henry said, "No offense, Vlad, but you've uttered that exact phrase every Friday since the first day of school. And you still haven't called her."

Vlad chewed his bottom lip thoughtfully. "Well, today's different."

Joss and Henry flashed him similar looks of disbelief.

Vlad sighed. They were probably right. After all, today really wasn't any different from any other day, apart from being a Friday, which was probably about the best day of the week, next to Saturday. He still had no idea what to say to Meredith. But it's the thought that counts.

After a quick walk home, Vlad made his way up the steps and in the front door, and then dropped his backpack near the stairs with a thump. "Aunt Nelly? You home?"

Nelly called from the kitchen, "In here, dear."

Nelly was by the counter, ripping fresh green herbs into bits and adding them to the pot on the stove. She wiped her hands on a towel and handed Vlad a thick, parchment envelope. "This came for you earlier."

Vlad stared at the envelope for a moment and then smiled. Just the pick-me-up he needed.

He took it from her, tore the envelope open, and sat at the table to read.

Dearest Vladimir,

It is with high spirits that I sit down to write this letter. I may have a solution to your recent mind-control troubles, but let me first express my great enthusiasm with your recent telepathic success! Your telepathy seems to be developing wonderfully, Vladimir. I couldn't be more proud. However, reading the minds of young ladies is certainly no way to get to know women at all.

Now, on to the reason that I am writing today.

I've already spoken to Nelly and she has granted permission for you to join me in December, when I travel to Siberia, Russia. We will travel to visit with an old, very dear friend of mine (and your father), by the name of Vikas. Do you recall my mention of the oldest vampire I know? This is him. I've arranged for Vikas to act as private tutor to you during our week-long stay. If he can't teach you how to influence the thoughts and actions of those around you, no one can. I know that you will make me very proud, Vladimir. And, though he has passed on, I'm certain that your father would be proud as well.

While in Siberia, I will have further business to attend to. This business concerns you, Vladimir, as well as the incident that occurred last spring in Elysia. I will explain further when I see you. Attached you will

*find a list of what to pack for our trip. I look forward
to seeing you in December!*

    Yours in Eternity,
    Otis

Vlad read the closing again and then looked up at Nelly. "When did you talk to Otis?"

Nelly glanced at the calendar. "Oh, I'd say it was about a week ago."

He threw Nelly an incredulous glance. "Why didn't you tell me he called?"

"You weren't home, sweetie. And I didn't tell you that he'd called because I knew how upset you'd be that you missed his call."

Vlad pursed his lips in a frown. It was the second time in three months that Otis had conveniently called while he was at school. "So I get to go with him over break?"

Nelly smiled. "We'll need to go shopping first, but yes. You can go."

Vlad tucked the letter inside his pocket and, reaching into the freezer for a bag of A negative, allowed himself a smile.

Vlad squinted up, blocking the glow of the streetlights with his hand. Otis was standing on the edge of a very tall building, looking down at him with wide, panic-stricken eyes. Blood dripped from a cut on Otis's forehead. He wiped it away with his sleeve, smearing it across his pale skin. "Vladimir, run! Run and don't look back!"

But Vlad wasn't about to turn his back on family. He focused hard on his body and willed it upward, shooting higher and faster than he ever had before. He stepped nimbly onto the building's roof and pulled Otis back from the edge. Otis shook his head and pleaded through his tears. "Please go, Vlad. You have no idea what he's capable of."

Vlad looked across the rooftop to the shadowy figure standing there. He squeezed Otis's shoulder. "This isn't your fight, Otis. It's mine."

But then Vlad was hit in the side and knocked to the ground. His knee smacked the tarred roof and cracked audibly. He winced and swore aloud.

Vlad glanced up at his uncle and saw Otis's eyes grow wide. He looked back to the shadow man, but his vision blurred and turned red, like blood.

He gasped, and the scene before him went black.

Sitting up in bed with beads of cool sweat clinging to his forehead, Vlad kicked the sheets from their tangled place around his feet. He shook the nightmare from his thoughts and glanced at the clock. It was two in the morning, still black as pitch outside. He slipped on his clothes quietly before grabbing his shoes and sunblock—just in case he was out later than he planned to be—then slid the Lucis into his back pocket and slipped out of his bedroom door to the library. Once he made it downstairs, he stopped in the kitchen to grab a snack and then went outside without waking up Nelly, or Amenti, Nelly's fat, fluffy, black cat.

Sometimes you just have to be alone to think, and sometimes the best place for thinking isn't home.

He had no idea what Otis had planned for him in Siberia, or whether or not he'd get along with a vampire he'd never met before. Other than Otis and his dad, he hadn't had much luck in that regard. What if Vikas didn't like him? Or worse, what if Vlad didn't like Vikas? It would be really hard to learn about vampire skills from a guy he couldn't stand sharing breathing space with.

Vlad released a nervous sigh and crossed the street. The moon hung full in the sky. It was golden, as if someone had dipped it in honey. His path to Bathory High was well lit and unoccupied. Thank glob for small favors, as his Aunt Nelly would say.

After reaching the back of the building, and making sure he hadn't been followed, he paused to listen to the goth kids who were gathered on the front steps. A girl's voice rose above the others. "I'm telling you, Sprat, it's haunted. That's why they closed the old church. This preacher just went nuts back in the 1800s and started killing people when they came in for confession. He did away with three whole families before they caught him, kids and all. Some even say he drank their blood out of the communion chalice."

Vlad suppressed a chuckle. He'd heard this story before, from Henry's older brother, Greg. It was just another tool for the upperclassmen to mess with the incoming freshmen. Usually, the story was accompanied by some kid dressed like a vampiric priest jumping out of the shadows. Greg had assured him that that was the worst of it—a quick scare, a few laughs, and life would go on. All the freshmen had to pay their dues. This was just one of the many collection methods.

Vlad peeked around the corner at the goth kids and smiled. If only they knew there was a *real* blood drinker among them.

The girl sighed with a note of irritation. "If you don't believe me, just wait and watch."

Vlad looked around to make sure no one could see him, and then concentrated until his body lifted from the ground. Levitating: not quite as cool as having a driver's license and your own car, but a close second.

For a moment, he had the urge to descend on the goths, fangs fully elongated, asking them in a spooky, gravelly voice how long it had been since their last confession. Despite how funny their reactions might be, he thought better of it and floated up four floors to the abandoned belfry of Bathory High, stepping in through one of the open arches.

Moonlight poured through the arched windows, lighting the way for Vlad to locate his lighter and candles. He crammed three into wax-covered candlesticks and lit them before flopping onto his dad's old office chair and running his fingers over the soft leather. It hadn't been easy getting the chair up to the belfry. He'd managed to wheel it from his old house to the high school without much trouble, but lugging the large chair up four stories while levitating had proven challenging, to say the least. In the end, he'd sworn A LOT, and then taken a screwdriver to the chair. After it was split into five pieces, he'd carried each piece up separately and reassembled it in the belfry.

It was tough but well worth it. After all, every bloodsucking fiend needs a sanctuary. And if Dracula could have a coffin, Vlad could have a comfy chair.

Lining the wall to his left were several stacks of various books he'd brought here to help pass the midnight hour. Most were older, classic novels—like *Alice's Adventures in Wonderland*, which had seriously freaked Vlad out as a kid and still did. Who wouldn't be scared by the tale of a girl falling into a bizarre world infested with talking animals and a queen with a thirst for blood?

Well, the queen, at least, Vlad could relate to.

But several of the books were from newer authors, and quite a few had been banned in both the school and the town library. Vlad couldn't understand the logic behind banning books. Tell kids they can't do something and then be surprised that your efforts drove them to do whatever you didn't want them to? Some grown-ups could be so inherently stupid. Try banning homework sometime. You might start seeing those straight A's so many parents long for.

Vlad shook his head. What was he thinking?

Atop the nearest stack of books sat a leather journal engraved *The Chronicles of Tomas Tod*—his dad's journal. Since he found it last year, Vlad had read the diary over a hundred times and could now recite passages from it by heart. Beneath it lay Vlad's own journal, in which he scribbled his private thoughts and experiences, hoping in some small way to emulate his father. The composition notebook he used as a journal was nearly full of entries and frayed at the edges, but Vlad hadn't saved up enough cash to buy a refillable leather version yet.

On the stack next to the journals was a framed photo. Vlad smiled at the photograph within. "Hey, Dad."

He pulled a snack pack out of the brown crumpled bag he'd been carrying and then fished around inside for the spoon he'd taken from the kitchen. His fangs elongated at the scent of blood, and he did nothing to will them back inside his gums. Sometimes, you just gotta let it all hang out.

He peeled the plastic wrap from the top of the small, plastic container and scooped a big spoonful of slushy blood into his mouth. The smell of late summer roses drifted in through the open arches from Mrs. Kipling's award-winning flower garden across the street. Vlad relaxed back into his dad's chair and finished his snack—his thoughts never far from what Otis had told him the last time they spoke regarding his late-night rendezvous, that D'Ablo had many friends, so to be on his guard.

And Vlad *had* been on his guard. He spent his entire summer looking over his shoulder and making sure he wasn't being followed by anyone with fangs. It was exhausting. There had been no sign whatsoever of vengeful vampires on the prowl in Bathory. He was beginning to think Otis was paranoid.

He ran a finger across inside of the plastic container and licked it clean.

On the floor beside his dad's old chair lay the book Otis had insisted he read—the *Compendium of Conscentia*. But Vlad had affectionately begun referring to it as the *Encyclopedia Vampyrica*. It was several inches thick. On its cover were a strange symbol and two locks that could not be opened with a key. He picked it up and placed his hand on the book's cover. The glyph on the book, as well as the tattooed symbol on the inside of his left wrist—two straight lines with three slashes between them, all encased in what looked like parentheses—glowed brightly, and the locks clicked open with ease.

He flipped to the sticky note about a third of the way into the book and read the second paragraph with halting clarity.

A multitude of vampiric councils guard and keep Elysia and bound our brethren to each of the three-hundred-and-thirteen laws. Each council is composed of a president, vice president, secretary, academic affairs officer, incident control officer, events coordinator, and treasurer. The Elysian laws were laid out by the original Elysian council, which formed in the early Paleolithic period—gifting us with power in numbers and the societal requirement of law and order.

Vlad sighed. Even vampire history was boring.

He flipped back several pages to another sticky note and ran his finger over a word that had continually surfaced in the book. Otis had told him time and time again not to concern himself with it. But there was a problem with that. Vlad was already quite concerned with the word.

Pravus.

Last year, as he perched in a tree above the heads of Otis and D'Ablo, Vlad had heard D'Ablo refer to him as the Pravus. He hadn't thought of it much at the time, but several passages referring to the Pravus in the vampire text had sent Vlad's imagination wandering. He'd thrown himself into his studies and could almost read the Elysian code without any trouble at all, but still those passages eluded him. Almost as if he wasn't supposed to be reading them.

The voice of the goth girl drifted in through the windows. "Kristoff! Andrew didn't mean it."

"Oh, he meant it. And he can bite me!"

At this, Vlad's ears perked up. Apparently, Andrew was this year's priest. Vlad crept out onto the ledge.

The goth kids were no longer sitting in their usual spot on the steps. Now the tall, silvery-haired goth was standing over the smallest of the group—a boy with mesh gloves and spiky hair that drooped slightly at the ends. Vlad crouched, perching on the ledge, and leaned forward a bit. The goth girl was standing beside the other two, with her pale hands held out pleadingly between the two boys. A fourth goth was slouching against the light post, watching the scene with an air of disinterest.

The boy on the ground shrugged. "Sorry, Kristoff. I didn't think you'd take it so personally."

"I'm not taking any crap from you, Andrew!" The silver-haired goth straightened and stepped back, slipping his hands into his trench coat's pockets. "Save your stupid pranks for Sprat. Not me."

Vlad chuckled and moved back inside. Kristoff, huh? That's funny. When Vlad and Kristoff were in the seventh grade, his name had been David and his hair had been blond.

Vlad squeezed his eyes shut and opened them again, suppressing a yawn, and then flipped open the book again and continued where he'd left off.

All of Elysia is bound to the same laws. Crimes are reported to the nearest council, and prisoners are held

until their trial, where evidence will be examined and they will be given the opportunity to defend themselves. If a member is found guilty of breaking a law, they shall be subject to whatever punishment their ruling council deems fitting.

Common forms of punishment are lashes by a leather whip, banishment, and community service. Death sentences are far more brutal—examples of this are dismemberment, excessive exposure to sunlight, being drained of all blood by another vampire, and being drawn and quartered by four stallions of the council's choosing.

After the trial, a blood party follows, where the prisoner's punishment is carried out and the participating council and witnesses celebrate the glory of Elysia by consuming mass quantities of the best human blood available, followed by slices of sponge cake. This tradition goes back to the invention of sponge cake, which had been a favorite of then council president, Peter Plogojowitz.

Bored with his studies, Vlad withdrew Otis's letter from his pocket and read it over again, as well as the enclosed list, which had a smaller, hastily scribbled note on the bottom.

Please be careful, Vladimir. My associates inform me that a vampire slayer may be headed for Bathory. Lay low. Don't tell Nelly, I'd hate to alarm her (and sharing further information with her about the ways of

Elysia would be criminal), and don't go anywhere
alone—bring your drudge with you at all times.
   —O

Vlad read over the note several times. On his third pass, the weight of his uncle's words slammed against his chest, stealing his breath.

He was being hunted.

He read the note one more time and glanced nervously around the belfry, then blew out the candle and sat in the dark until his eyes adjusted to the dim light of the moon.

The fact the vampire slayers actually existed might have been something Otis could have mentioned as a nasty possibility before he drove off at the beginning of the summer. Or even at the beginning of his letter. Something about a stake-carrying jerk with a hatred of vampires didn't strike Vlad as a P.S. kind of thing. It was pretty crucial information, considering Vlad was Bathory's only resident blood drinker.

Until Otis's warning, Vlad had confined his belief in vampire slayers to movies and television. After all, who would believe in a guy who stalks the night with a crucifix and a wooden stake? Might as well believe in werewolves or the boogeyman. The idea that a person might exist who hunted and killed vampires, for whatever reason, sent his stomach flip-flopping. The best thing he could do was to keep to himself and familiar faces. If a slayer was headed for Bathory, he might not even notice Vlad. If he did . . .

Vlad shivered.

He folded the letter, slid it back into the envelope, and hoped that Otis would return to Bathory before the slayer could become an issue.

He kissed the tips of his fingers and touched his hand to the picture of his dad. He looked around the dark room once before stepping out onto the ledge and floating down to the ground. He was tempted to take to the treetops in order to avoid bumping into anyone who might be looking to impale him with a wooden stake, but he felt kind of tired. The last thing Vlad needed was to fall from a tree. While Vlad healed at an abnormally fast rate, it still hurt whenever he got scrapes and bruises. The rib D'Ablo had broken last year had been no picnic, either. Six days of almost constant pain.

It had felt like an eternity.

Vlad floated down to the ground, rubbed his eyes with the heels of his hands, and yawned. From the corner of his eye, he thought he saw a flicker of lightning, but when he looked up, all he could see were clear skies. The sensation that he was being watched crept up his spine like cold, skeletal fingers. He dropped his hands and looked around, but he didn't have to look hard. A dark figure was standing across the street, his eyes on Vlad.

The slayer.

Vlad had to will his body to keep still and not bolt down the street in a screeching panic. It was very likely the guy was just out for a late-night stroll, wondering what a kid his age was doing hanging out at the high school at almost two in the morning. Perfectly normal. Nothing to worry about.

But just to be sure . . .

Vlad pushed with his mind. Suddenly he was standing across from the school, watching a boy who was most certainly not a boy. *Yes . . . this is the one. And once I have his blood . . .*

Vlad felt a strange *crunch* in his head and pulled out of the man's thoughts. His head throbbed in time with his racing heart. He looked across the street again, but the vampire slayer was nowhere to be found.

He took off at a sprint around the corner and headed toward home, all the while cursing himself for not checking if there was a chapter in his book on slayers and how to defend oneself. His feet were moving so fast, he felt like he was flying. After a quick glance down, just to be sure he wasn't, he looked around at the familiar houses. He was almost home. He rounded the tree on the corner . . .

. . . and ran face-first into a warm body, knocking the person to the ground.

Joss looked up at Vlad. "In a hurry?"

Vlad helped him up and shook his head. "Kind of. If Nelly catches me out this late, I'll be grounded for the rest of my life. What are you doing out here, anyway? You scared the crap out of me."

Joss gestured to his backpack on the ground with a nod. "I was collecting bugs."

Vlad raised a curious eyebrow. "And filling your back-pack with them?"

Joss laughed. "Kind of. I'm thinking of becoming an entomologist when I'm older. I like collecting insects and watching them for a few days, learning about them. I have a bunch of jars in my backpack. I set the bugs free when I'm done, though."

"Not a killer, huh?" Vlad forced a laugh, so relieved that Joss hadn't been the creepy guy across the street who'd been thinking about Vlad's blood.

Joss just stared at him.

"You are one weird kid, Joss." Vlad had hoped to make Joss smile, but instead, Joss just looked uncomfortable.

He slugged Joss in the shoulder. "But not as weird as me. At least you have interesting hobbies. All I do is read."

That did it. A smile crossed Joss's face. "Well, I read, too. So who's weirder?"

Vlad thought about it for a moment, and then nodded. He and Joss both spoke at the same time. "Henry."

Joss hoisted his backpack over his shoulder, the heavy jars weighing it down. "So what are you doing out in the middle of the night?"

Vlad shrugged. "I guess I'm more of a night person."

After a moment, Joss smiled. "Me, too."

8
SECRETS EXPOSED

VLAD KNOCKED SOFTLY on Nelly's door. "Nelly, I'm leaving soon."

Her response was slow, heavy with sleep. "Okay. I'll be right down."

He listened at her door for another moment until he heard her get out of bed. Sometimes, when she'd just worked a late shift, he felt bad about making sure she was up before he left the house. But after what happened to his parents, the superstitious part of him insisted that he couldn't leave anyone sleeping while he went off to school.

Downstairs he dropped his backpack on the kitchen table beside his sunblock. Stretching in the early-morning light, he retrieved a bag of blood from the fridge and glanced at the phone.

There it was, mocking him. Pointing out the fact that it was ridiculous the way he was brave enough to face a killer vampire last year, but too chicken to call Meredith and say he was sorry for not kissing her when she'd clearly wanted him to. Well . . . maybe she hadn't, but Vlad couldn't think of any other reason for her to lean toward him with her eyes closed and lips puckered like that. He chewed his bottom lip thoughtfully for a moment before reaching for the phone. Before he could overthink his actions, he picked it up and dialed.

Riiiiing . . .

Vlad's heart skipped a beat, then knocked hard on his insides, as if trying to wake him from whatever bout of insanity had taken him in its grasp.

Riiiiing . . .

His heart settled some. Maybe she wasn't home. Maybe he'd just have to try back later. Maybe—

"Hello?"

His heart punched him in the chest once, as if to say it had told him so. "Hi. This is—"

"Vlad?" Her tone sounded more curious than angry, something he couldn't be more grateful for.

"Yeah. I just wanted to call and . . ." He wrinkled his forehead. Why had he wanted to call? Other than hearing her voice, what else was there? He had to have a reason. ". . . and ask you . . ."

"Ask me what?"

Vlad swallowed the lump in his throat and spoke before the little voice at the back of his head could tell him not to. "I wanted to ask you if you had a date to the Snow Ball yet."

Meredith was quiet for a moment. "Vlad, are you asking me out?"

Vlad cleared his throat. Twice. Then he mumbled something unintelligible. Then he coughed.

"It's just that . . . well, I already have a date to the Snow Ball." She paused and then lowered her voice to a near whisper. "You know, when you didn't call after the Freedom Fest dance, I wasn't sure you were still interested in going out with me. So, I asked someone else."

Vlad panicked. "I was just asking for a . . . a friend."

"Oh. I'm sorry. I thought that—"

He forced a laugh. "Me? Go to a semiformal dance? That's just nuts. I have way too much stuff to do. Anyway, I guess I'll see ya around."

"Yeah . . . see ya."

She'd barely finished her sentence before Vlad placed the phone back in its cradle.

His heart deflated, along with any hope that he would ever get a second chance with the girl of his dreams. The center of his chest ached, and for a moment, Vlad wondered if his heart had actually broken into a thousand pieces. But when he placed his hand against his chest, he could still feel its beats. They were slower, as if his heart had been through a lot in the last few minutes. But it was still working.

Vlad bit into the bag and sucked until it was empty, then tossed it into the biohazard container beneath the sink. He grabbed his backpack and headed for the front door. It was weird that Henry had been walking to school without him, due to some early-morning student council meetings. Weirder still that Vlad had someone other than Henry to hang out with.

Vlad noticed somebody moving on the front porch—he could see them through the window. He smiled and opened the front door, stepping out into the morning sun. If it wasn't for Joss, Vlad's mornings over the past couple of weeks would have been rather lonely. "Hey, Joss."

"Hey, Vlad. You ready?"

Vlad sighed and adjusted the strap of his backpack. "As ever."

They wound their way between houses until they came to Bathory High. Vlad looked up at the school and groaned. "Why can't it be Friday?"

"Because it's Tuesday." Joss chuckled.

Stephanie Brawn skipped over and smiled.

She wasn't smiling at Vlad, of course. But she was smiling.

"Hey, Joss. You want a copy of the school paper?" Her tone was so sickly sweet that Vlad nearly vomited. He'd never realized how much he really despised Stephanie . . . until he heard her speak.

Joss smiled back. "Sure."

Vlad mumbled, "Catch you later, Joss."

He wandered up the steps before Stephanie could speak again.

The weatherman had predicted snow, so Vlad wasn't sure what so many kids were doing outside, and he *really* wasn't sure why they were each paying a bizarre amount of attention to the school newspaper. Nobody ever read that rag. Well, apart from the jocks and cheerleaders, who took great joy in the fact that at least one of them was featured on every page.

He made his way to the top step and paused, looking back over his shoulder. Several people were huddled together; he could hear them talking about something, but not about what.

With a shiver, Vlad hurried into the school and headed for his locker. The students inside were also paying annoyingly close attention to the paper. By the time Vlad saw Henry, his nerves had tangled into a large bunch in the middle of his stomach, but he wasn't sure why. He gestured to the crowd of paper-reading students. "What's up?"

Henry's face was pale. His eyes were bigger than Vlad had ever seen them. He shook his head, held a copy of the paper up for Vlad's perusal, and said, "Apparently, you are."

On the front page was a blurry black-and-white photo of someone floating in midair, right in front of the school's belfry.

Vlad's heart stopped. Then it picked up the pace at three times its normal rate.

He shook his head. "Who took this?"

Henry pointed to the accompanying article. "It looks like you have a shadow."

Vlad relaxed his arm until his backpack dropped to the floor. He leaned with his back against his locker and read the title aloud. "'A Monster in Bathory? By Eddie Poe, freshman correspondent.'"

Vlad swore under his breath, but as his eyes scanned the rest of the article, he realized that Eddie was more of a problem than he'd thought. Eddie rambled about monsters, "inhuman beasts with purple eyes" that were invading the small town of Bathory.

Apparently, Eddie hadn't forgotten about Vlad's eyes flashing on Halloween night.

True to Henry's theory, Eddie *had* been following him. He'd gotten close enough to Vlad to spy him leaving the belfry one night, and Vlad hadn't even noticed the camera flash. So much for extrasensory powers. What good was being half-vampire if Vlad couldn't tell when a clumsy geek with a camera was following him around? He finished the article and cursed aloud. His fangs pushed their way forcefully out of his gums, and he clamped his mouth shut to hide them.

That was the last thing he needed.

He scanned the photo again. It was grainy, gray, and dark. In fact, if Vlad didn't know that he was actually capable of floating he might not have believed the photo was of him at all. It might have been a branch. A very pale, good-looking branch.

Vlad folded the paper with a grunt. "I think Eddie and I need to have a little talk."

Henry nodded. "I thought so. He's in the library."

Vlad raised an eyebrow before turning to open his locker. "Hiding out? You'd think he'd be strutting some over ruining my life, or maybe swapping stories with Bill and Tom— they all seem to be on the same side now."

"Your life isn't ruined. Nobody believes him. It's a joke. I mean, if it had been anybody else on the paper staff, they might think twice. But Eddie?" Henry forced a laugh. "The guy's scared of his own shadow. He probably still sleeps with a night-light."

Vlad dropped his backpack inside the locker and muttered, "What if somebody does believe him, Henry? All it takes is one or two and my cover is blown. Nelly would freak. Otis would be furious. Not to mention what the population of Bathory might think of having me around gorging on the blood of innocents."

"Hey, as far as you know, that blood came from some psycho killer. Nelly has no control over who donates your dinner."

Vlad shook his head. His heart hadn't let up since he saw the newspaper. "That's not the point, Henry. What if—"

"Vlad." Henry locked eyes with him. "Everything's going to be fine. Trust me on this, okay?"

Suddenly, Vlad felt a lot better. No matter what happened, at least Henry had his back. He nodded, and his muscles relaxed some. When he pulled his hand away from his locker, the metal was dented in. He and Henry stared at it in confusion for a minute, and then Henry cleared his throat and asked, "You still want to talk to Eddie?"

"Absolutely." Vlad shut his locker, still wondering how he managed to bend the door, and turned to make his way to the library.

A loud, deep voice boomed over the PA system. "Edgar Poe, report to the principal's office IMMEDIATELY! Edgar Poe. Right now, young man."

Vlad and Henry exchanged glances before pushing their way quickly through the crowd to the principal's office. From the hall, they heard Principal Hardwick chewing out Eddie. Most of what they heard were loud, low sounds of yelling, but every once in a while, a word would come through loud and clear. "...irresponsible ... never in all my days ... you're lucky I don't ... childish antics ... call your parents ...

ridiculous notions . . . wasting my time . . . two weeks' detention . . . apology, young man!"

After a moment of silence, the office door opened, and Eddie made his way slowly into the hall, his eyes downcast.

The anger that had built up in Vlad's chest subsided some. Not a lot. But some. It was replaced by pity.

Eddie's cheeks were blushing bright red. He looked humiliated. Defeated, even. He clutched the camera that was hanging from his neck with both hands and let the office door close on its own.

Vlad's fangs shrank back. There wasn't anything he could do or say to Eddie that hadn't already been done or said. Sure, he was still mad about the possibility of being exposed. But he was madder at himself than at Eddie—he was the one who hadn't been careful. Eddie had just been looking for a way to be special, to be noticed in any way that could be deemed good.

Realizing he was being watched, Eddie looked up. The moment he caught Vlad in his sights, the embarrassment in his features disappeared, replaced by determination.

And that's when Vlad realized that it didn't matter if he told Eddie he'd been acting crazy, or that nobody at Bathory High believed his article to be any more valid than those in the *Weekly World News*, or that Vlad had been nice to Eddie ever since they first met in kindergarten. Eddie was determined to explore the depths of Vlad's secret and expose him for the inhuman creature he was.

Vlad didn't need to read his mind to see that. It was all there in Eddie's determined glare.

Eddie nodded once, and then shuffled down the hall.

Vlad watched him and then turned to Henry. "I have a problem, Henry."

Henry sighed, watching Eddie, too. "Yeah. And his name is Eddie Poe."

9
SNOWFLAKES AND MEMORIES

VLAD OPENED HIS BOOK for the twenty-third time and snapped it closed again. Music thumped in a continuous rhythm, shaking the flame of his candle. How could he expect to focus on reading when several floors below, in Bathory High's gym, Meredith was likely twirling around the dance floor at the annual Snow Ball with her handsome, charming, what-a-swell-guy date? And Vlad, who'd been too chicken to even approach the thought of asking Meredith out again, was left alone and dateless while his two best friends were busy downstairs with dates of their own. It was a rather pathetic situation to be in, so Vlad did the next best thing to attending the semiformal dance alone—he went to his secret sanctuary in the belfry to mope.

Vlad had every right to mope. Henry had scored a date with a pretty blonde junior whose twin sister happened to have an enormous crush on Henry's brother, Greg. Joss had been even luckier than Henry, as he'd managed to score a date with the prettiest girl in the entire town.

Not that he deserved it. Not that anyone deserved a night out with Meredith Brookstone.

For about two seconds after hearing that Joss would be taking Meredith to the dance, Vlad hated them both with a deep passion. Then he felt an immediate mixture of guilt, stupidity, and self-loathing. Vlad should have asked Meredith to the dance weeks ago. But after their last date, he didn't have much hope in the world that she'd actually say yes anyway.

Vlad tried keeping quiet about his feelings, but every time Joss would ask him if he could believe that Meredith had asked him out, Vlad screamed *NO!* inside his skull. And Joss couldn't seem to take a hint. So finally, he'd snapped back one day at lunch that no, he couldn't believe she'd actually asked him out, because who in their right mind thinks anthropologists are hot?

Joss had sulked the rest of the day, but Vlad wasn't about to apologize. Joss had broken the biggest friend code there was: thou shalt not date the girl that thy best friend has a crush on.

All Vlad knew was that if Meredith's name popped up in the next "who's the better kisser" discussion at the lunch table, he might lose it all over his newest friend.

He leaned back in his chair and listened to the music drifting in through the arched windows. His breath formed small clouds of fog in front of his lips. The belfry was freezing, but he wasn't in the mood to sit at home and watch Nelly busy herself with holiday baking. Besides, the idea that he was probably the only person besides Eddie Poe who hadn't gone to the dance had made him feel particularly mopey—so, vampire slayer or not, Vlad had gripped the Lucis in his hand and threw glances over his shoulder at every tree, every bush, the entire way here.

He'd finished packing for the big winter break trip that afternoon, but there had been no further word from Otis, so he wasn't sure yet whether or not his packing was in vain. Rather than stay home and pace (not to mention mope), he'd come here to eavesdrop in the freezing cold.

So far, it wasn't doing much to calm his nerves.

Vlad held his hands up to the candlelight for warmth. The buckles on the backs of his fingerless gloves shined in the low light. Beside him, his father's portrait watched with a smile. The candle's flame shrank and, with a brief burst of light, went out. It was as if the belfry were telling him it was time to give up moping and go home. Vlad whispered into the shadows, to whatever ghosts might be listening, "I can take a hint."

He glanced over the ledge before stepping out of one of the archways and hovering slowly to a tree near the parking lot. From there he made his way to the cement. He couldn't leave footsteps in the snow that seemed to come out of nowhere, especially not coming from the belfry. It's the little things that get you in trouble.

The snow crunched under his shoes as he made his way around to the front of the school. Vlad might be cold, but his curiosity had not yet been quenched.

Two couples stood just inside the double doors. He recognized Henry right away, despite the fact that Henry's face was buried in a scary-looking kiss with the blonde junior. They looked to be attached by suction cups that had been affixed to their faces. Try as they might to break free, Henry and the junior were trapped. And Vlad was pretty sure they were happy with their predicament.

But it was possible that they were attempting to gnaw each other's lips off. Vlad wondered for a moment if any of his vampiric nature had rubbed off when he and Henry were eight.

The other couple was standing in shadows, not kissing, but clearly standing very close. The girl glanced over her shoulder, toward Vlad, and with a word to her date, who nodded and headed back toward the gym, Meredith opened the double doors and stepped outside.

Vlad's feet were frozen to the sidewalk, but it wasn't due to snow or ice.

Meredith pulled her satin shawl over her porcelain shoulders and, with a shiver, managed a small smile. "Hi, Vlad."

Vlad cleared his throat and looked down at his feet and over at the doors—anything but into her perfect eyes. "Hey."

Meredith folded her arms in front of herself. Had she really braved the cold just to say hi to him? Vlad knew he should say something, but he wasn't sure what exactly. He'd narrowed it down to either something involving the weather or school, when she parted her pretty pink lips and asked, "Can I ask you something?"

Vlad smirked. "You just did."

"Yeah, but I meant . . ." Meredith bit her lip and glanced over her shoulder at the door. Henry and the junior were still attached at the face. "Never mind."

The sight of her turning away gave Vlad a shot of bravery that he desperately needed. "No, what is it?"

Meredith's cheeks were blushing, but Vlad couldn't tell if it was from embarrassment or the intense cold. "Don't you like me, Vlad? I mean, after Freedom Fest last year, you just sort of avoided me. And then you didn't ask me to the Snow Ball. Did I do something wrong? I mean . . . besides asking Joss to the dance to make you jealous?" She shivered and looked at him with pleading eyes.

Vlad's eyes widened a bit. She'd tried to make him jealous. So that's why she'd asked Joss to the dance. Man, had it worked.

He took off his jacket and held it out for her. With a grateful nod, she slipped her arms into its sleeves. Vlad shivered against the cold but couldn't help but smile. The sight of Meredith's smooth skin sliding against the insides of his jacket was enough to keep him warm for at least the next few minutes. "You didn't do anything wrong."

Meredith's hair was swept up away from her face. Tiny curls stuck out here and there, pinned in place by miniature rhinestone snowflakes. Real snowflakes joined them on the background of Meredith's lush chocolate hair. Vlad felt his heart squeeze its way up through his chest and settle in his throat. Meredith dropped her eyes to the ground between them. "So what is it?"

Vlad swallowed hard, but his heart refused to budge. "I don't know."

She met his eyes. Vlad swore he could see the threat of tears in hers. "Are you sure you don't know? Or is it like Chelsea Whitaker says, that you don't think I'm pretty enough to go out with? Because I like you, Vlad. I really like you."

Vlad wrinkled his forehead in confusion. Why on earth would Chelsea Whitaker think she knew anything at all about Vlad when the expanse of their interaction had been Chelsea making snide comments about Vlad and pulling stupid pranks that always seemed to land Vlad in detention? That sealed it. There was no way Vlad was ever going to be able to comprehend the complexities of teenage girls.

Meredith must have taken his blank, astonished stare for something that it wasn't, as she turned abruptly and rushed up the steps toward the double doors. Five more steps and she'd be through the door and on her way to Joss's arms. Vlad blurted, "I like you, too."

Meredith stopped and turned around.

"I don't know, because this is still kinda new to me. You're the first girl I've ever asked out. I guess I didn't know the rules as well as I should have." He swallowed hard and ran his tongue over his incisors. How could she like him? He was such a freak. Not to mention dangerous. Nelly had always said that women like a dangerous man. Was that it? On some level, could she detect the danger of him, and that's what she found so appealing? Or maybe, Vlad thought, it was nothing at all. "Maybe it was smart, asking Joss to the dance instead of me. But one thing's for sure . . . Chelsea's wrong. You're the prettiest girl I've ever seen."

After a pause, she gestured with a bent finger for Vlad to come closer. Vlad booked it up the stairs and nearly fell. Twice.

She laughed and brushed some snow from his blushing cheek.

Her fingers against his skin were all he needed to label this evening well spent, but then Meredith leaned closer and said, "You're sweet, Vlad."

He was going to say that she was sweet, too, and he meant it when he'd called her pretty, that he had wanted to be the one to take her to the Snow Ball, but he'd been too scared that she'd say no. But there was no time. Meredith pressed her lips to his.

A moment that probably only lasted a total of two seconds stretched on into eternity in Vlad's mind. His heart had continued its journey north and slid out his ear—he was pretty sure it was now floating several feet above their heads. Just like that, the cold was gone. Meredith Brookstone had kissed him, and the world was right again.

She walked up the steps and pulled the door open. Vlad saw her smile in his direction before the doors squeaked closed. He reached up and brushed his lips with his fingertips. His whispered words were a gray cloud in the cold air. "Thank you."

After several minutes spent in front of the high school, staring at the doors in blissful contemplation, Vlad turned and started home. He was halfway there when he realized that Meredith hadn't returned his jacket.

Shivering, Vlad quickened his pace and squinted into the blowing snow. By the time he reached his house, his fingers had numbed, and his arms felt frozen to his sides. But his lips were still warm from Meredith's kiss.

He was crossing the street when he noticed a man standing on the corner, watching the house.

Vlad's heart shot back into his body and grabbed onto his ribs for support.

The slayer.

Vlad bolted across the street, toward the house. In a blink, he had the Lucis out of his jeans pocket and his thumb poised over the end—he wasn't sure what good it would do him against a human, but it was all he had. He hurried to get inside, both to protect Nelly from a madman and to get warm before he could formulate a plan. Maybe they could hide out in Stokerton for a while. Or, considering how unpopular Vlad probably was with Elysia for blowing a hole through their president last year, maybe not. He opened the gate and rushed toward the house but was stopped by a dark figure that entered his path. Vlad swore under his breath and pointed the Lucis at the slayer, but a strong hand gripped his wrist and pointed it into the distance. He looked up at the slayer's face, and his eyes widened in surprise.

"I'm glad to see you taking precautions, Vladimir. It's good to see you again." Otis's entire face smiled. His eyes, lips, cheeks, even his chin seemed to have a pleasant glow. He stepped forward and grabbed a stunned Vlad into a tight hug. When they pulled apart, Vlad thought he caught a glimmer of relief in his uncle's eyes . . . until Otis smirked with bemusement at Vlad's lips.

Vlad rubbed his mouth with the back of his hand. If Meredith had left glittered lip gloss on him, it was better that Otis saw it than Nelly. The last thing he needed was to be grounded for making out with a girl (not that he and Meredith were making out, but try explaining that to Nelly), when he was supposed to be sucking down sodas at Eat,

Bathory's one and only diner. Sure, the name of the restaurant was Aunt Polly's Dining Emporium, but nowhere on the front of the building was that listed. All it said, in big red and blue neon, was EAT.

Vlad breathed a sigh of relief. No slayer. Not yet, anyway. "Uncle Otis. You could've dropped me a note or called or something. I didn't think you were coming."

Otis raised a perplexed eyebrow. "Didn't you get my letter, inviting you to Siberia with me?"

Vlad shrugged. "Well, yeah. But that was a month ago. Where'd you go after that? I've got some questions I want to ask you about my abilities."

"Haven't you been reading the book on vampire history your father left behind?"

"Of course. But, Otis"—Vlad shook his head—"no book has all the answers. Besides, I've missed you. Where have you been?"

The smile returned to Otis's face. He placed a hand on Vlad's shoulder and squeezed. "I've missed you as well. As for where I've been . . . well, we'll discuss that inside."

As they turned toward the house, Vlad felt a strange nudge in his mind. He glanced at Otis and clamped down on his thoughts. His uncle wrinkled his brow before following Vlad up the steps. Vlad was about to ask why Otis had been attempting to examine his thoughts, when the door opened and a flushed Nelly welcomed them with a surprised smile and a plate of steaming cookies. "Otis?"

Vlad glanced at his uncle, whose eyes sparkled at Nelly. "How are you, Nelly? You look—"

"Cold? Because I'm cold." Vlad nudged passed his aunt and sat on the stairs, where he removed his shoes and waited for the hushed whispers to end.

Nelly glanced at Vlad. "Where's your jacket?"

Before Vlad could answer, Otis stepped inside and took the plate from Nelly. "Chocolate chip. My favorite. I wouldn't suppose you could spare a little something to warm me up before I indulge."

Minutes later, Otis, Nelly, and Vlad were sitting around the dining room table, sipping from china teacups. Vlad's cup matched Otis's in that each was filled with microwaved blood, but Otis had barely touched his, focusing more, in a way that sent Vlad's gag reflex crazy, on Nelly. As Nelly cleared the table, Vlad turned to Otis. "So, what have you been up to, traveling all over the world?"

The happy glimmer in Otis's eye faded, and it was clear his thoughts were in an unpleasant place. "I've been running, Vladimir. Running and trying to learn some things."

Vlad swallowed a lump of guilt. "Who have you been running from? Elysia? Is it because of helping me last year?"

"Partly, yes. D'Ablo had many followers, and I broke many laws by helping you. The punishment, should they catch me, would be a most painful death. But there are other things. Darker things that I will not speak of. Suffice it to say we should enjoy our time together, Vladimir. Good things only rarely last." Otis glanced over his shoulder at the window, as if suddenly fearful they weren't alone. Instinctively, Vlad looked, too, but he saw nothing. He guessed that Otis was watching for whatever ghosts were haunting his thoughts.

Vlad leaned in and whispered, "Otis, I need to know more about the slayer."

But Otis's eyes were fixed on the window. He stood with purpose and crossed the room quickly. After a careful survey of the scene outside the window, he sighed wearily and rested his forehead against the glass. "Snow. Just snow."

Vlad approached with careful steps and placed a hand on Otis's shoulder. "Maybe you should get some rest."

Without looking at him, Otis reluctantly shook his head. "No. You rest. You'll need it tomorrow. We leave at four in the morning."

Vlad opened his mouth to protest—after all, his uncle looked exhausted—but something in Otis's eyes when he glanced back at Vlad told him to keep his opinions to himself. He offered a nod and made his way slowly up the stairs. This wasn't exactly the reunion he'd hoped for.

Vlad lay on his bed and dozed in and out of sleep until a soft ball of fluff stepped on his forehead. With a grunt, he nudged Amenti off his face and sat up. The alarm clock glowed a cool blue 1:31. Vlad sat up and rubbed his eyes. His stomach rumbled its late-night demands, so he slipped out the door and downstairs for a snack.

The light in the living room was on. He peered around the corner, hoping to find Otis either snoring away on the couch or wide awake and ready to answer Vlad's questions about the slayer. What he found gave him pause.

Otis was sitting in the wingback chair, looking exhausted and sad. Nelly stood behind him and placed a hand on his shoulder. Otis covered her hand with his and squeezed. Each of them smiled wearily into the other's eyes, and as Vlad looked on, he couldn't help but smile, too. He'd never seen two people so immediately, unabashedly attracted to each other. Not since . . .

Vlad's smile slipped.

His eyes brimmed with tears.

Not since his parents.

The scene in front of him changed. Vlad was ten and up hours past his bedtime. He'd snuck down the hall to his father's study, where he'd spied his parents exchanging loving glances and holding hands. His mother had been standing behind his father in his favorite chair.

It was the last time he saw his parents alive.

The next morning, he'd risen early, turned off their alarms so they could sleep in, and gotten himself off to school. That afternoon he'd found them dead.

Vlad blinked away more tears. Nelly had draped a blanket over Otis, who, despite his will, was beginning to doze off.

Suddenly, Vlad didn't feel hungry anymore.

He went back upstairs and looked at the framed photo of his parents on the dresser before crawling under the covers. His mom and dad were smiling at him, but tonight their smiles seemed forced—almost as if they were trying to hide the pain of missing him. He tried to block out the memory of finding their charred remains, but the nightmarish experience rushed through the forefront of his mind with a whiff of ash and smoke.

Vlad hugged his pillow and stared at the photo of his parents and cried until sleep took him over at last.

10
SIBERIA

AFTER TWENTY-SIX HOURS on various planes that took
Vlad from Stokerton to New York, then Paris and after
that, Moscow, Vlad was about as exhausted as a person
could get. Everyone in the world seemed to be traveling
with him and Otis, as each airport had been exceedingly,
obnoxiously busy. On each plane Vlad had tried to nap,
but apparently, flight attendants are part bloodhound and
can sniff a sleeping person from a mile away. By their third
flight, he'd become convinced that it was written in their
flight attendant bylaws that if anyone within their reach on
an airplane begins to feel remotely drowsy, they should
offer them a drink . . . or some pretzels . . . or one of those

stupid little pillows that were barely big enough to cover Vlad's ear, let alone cushion his head against the window.

Otis had apparently no trouble snoozing his way from Moscow to Novosibirsk, Russia, as he'd snored quietly into Vlad's ear for roughly an hour before Vlad nudged him. Otis snorted and turned his head the other way, content to snore in the direction of the angry-looking woman across the aisle. Vlad watched out the window but couldn't see anything but clouds. His entire body felt alive with energy— soon he'd be getting instruction on telepathy from, what Otis had said, one of the oldest, most talented vampires around. The anticipation was making it increasingly difficult to keep still. He sighed and nudged Otis once more.

This time, Otis rubbed his eyes and sat up. "I must have dozed off. Did you get much sleep?"

Like a dog to a whistle, a thin flight attendant with brown hair tapped Otis on the shoulder. Vlad rolled his eyes before she could say, "Anything to drink, sir?"

He politely waved her away and turned back to Vlad, who shook his head. "Why are we going to Siberia? Isn't it cold there?"

"This time of year, yes, quite. But in the summer it's actually a rather warm and beautiful place." Otis smiled. His eyes twinkled, and for a moment, Vlad longed for a time when they could be together for good. Like a real family—he, Nelly, and Otis. He wondered if that time would ever come or if the vampires of Elysia had made some solemn vow that they would do everything in their power to make sure that Vlad's life would never be happy or even remotely normal.

As if he were reading Vlad's thoughts—which, Vlad reminded himself, might actually have been the case—Otis's voice broke through. "I'm sorry I've not seen you in so long, Vlad. Unfortunately, I have reasons for having kept my distance."

Vlad shrugged. "It's okay. I know you have stuff going on. And the letters have helped."

Otis looked hopeful. "Have they?"

Vlad nodded. "I mean, it would be better if I could use my telepathy to get a B in English, but . . ."

Otis chuckled. "Oh, the stories I could tell you about your father and the trouble we got into reading minds."

"So? Tell me."

To Vlad's surprise, Otis's cheeks blushed pink. "When you're older. Much older. Let's just say we got slapped a lot."

Vlad shook his head in bemusement. "What's Vikas like, anyway?"

"He's kind, warm, friendly, but stubborn." Otis smiled and shook his head. "Incredibly stubborn. And very talented—the finest teacher I've ever known."

Vlad nibbled on his bottom lip for a second. "Do you think he'll like me?"

Otis met his gaze with smiling eyes. "Vladimir, I do believe it would be impossible for Vikas not to like you. He adored Tomas, and you're very much like your father."

Vlad sighed happily and settled back in his seat. He wanted to ask his uncle about what it was like to live among other vampires, and other things—like why he couldn't read the Pravus passages in the *Encyclopedia Vampyrica*, and why Otis hadn't mentioned the reality of vampire slayers before—but the proximity of the other passengers made him a little uncomfortable when it came to talking openly about who and what he was.

He lay back and watched the gray clouds rush by beneath them. To his surprise, Otis shook him from unexpected sleep. They exited the plane and, after a long wait in the customs line, they wandered through the crowd to the brisk outdoors, where a taxi was waiting. Otis spoke something in Russian and handed the driver a colorful slip of paper with the number 500 on it. The driver held the paper out to him and uttered something that sounded like surprise, but Otis waved him away and placed their bags in the trunk.

It didn't take long before the cab came to a stop in front of a small building just outside Novosibirsk. Otis handed the driver another 500-ruble note, and the driver uttered something that must have meant "thank you" in Russian.

They stepped out of the cab, and Vlad pulled the collar of his new winter coat up around his neck and drew his hat down around his ears. He knew Siberia was supposed to be cold, but negative temperatures looked a whole lot warmer on a computer screen.

The door of the building opened and a man stepped out, dressed in layers of wool. A large hood covered his head, and though he wore a scarf over the lower half of his face, Vlad could tell he wasn't smiling. The man grumbled at Otis in Russian. Otis spoke with a friendly tone that turned slightly threatening. The man paused and glanced at Vlad. He nodded and led them around back, where a sled was waiting. Hitched to the front was a team of nine dogs. Vlad listened to Otis and the man debate something for a few minutes before approaching the largest dog in the front and holding out his gloved hand. The dog's ice blue eyes twinkled, and he nuzzled Vlad's hand.

Otis moved closer and scratched the dog behind the ear. "Beautiful animals, aren't they? Dmitri's family has been breeding huskies for years."

Vlad looked back at the man, who was watching them with squinted eyes and stuffing colorful slips of paper into his coat pocket. "Did you give him money?"

Otis nodded. "Twenty thousand rubles to rent the dogs and sled."

Vlad pulled his hand away from the dog and widened his eyes at his uncle. "That sounds like a lot."

Otis bent over to check the dogs' harnesses. "It works out to roughly seven hundred American dollars. A fair price, considering what I'm asking these dogs to do."

"What exactly are you asking them to do?" The wind had picked up, slicing through Vlad's layered clothes like a hot knife through butter. Vlad shivered and clenched his teeth.

Satisfied with the harnesses, Otis moved to the back of the sled, strapped their suitcases to a flat area there, and gestured for Vlad to sit on the rectangle of wood in front of him. "To take us to the hidden village of Elysia."

Vlad lowered himself onto the sled and drew a wool blanket over his legs. Otis had stepped onto the sled and was busy pulling his gloves tight over his fingers. He didn't seem bothered by the cold at all. Vlad pulled the blanket up to his nose and said, "But I thought Elysia was in Stokerton."

"Remember what I told you before? Elysia is anywhere our kind gather to share in one another's company. We're traveling to the hidden village of Elysia, home of the Siberian council." Otis called something out to the dogs, but Vlad didn't hear what he said. The wind had picked up again. It howled in his ears as he, Otis, and the dogs moved quickly over breathtaking terrain. They passed forests and mountains, gliding over miles and miles of snow. Vlad stayed huddled under his blanket. Neither he nor Otis spoke.

The sky turned black and stars rose high above them. Vlad could no longer feel his toes.

After what seemed like ages, Otis brought the dogs to a stop and stepped toward the crest of a hill. Two men were standing there, each covered from head to foot in many layers of fur. The three men conversed, and with a nod, Otis stepped over to Vlad. "Come. These men will care for the dogs. The village is just down this hill, in the valley below."

"When will I meet your friend?" Vlad strained to remember the name Otis had mentioned briefly in his letter.

"Vikas?" The corner of Otis's mouth rose in a smirk and his eyes moved to something behind Vlad. "You're about to."

With a somewhat nervous breath, Vlad turned and looked behind him.

A tall, broad-shouldered man approached from the edge of the forest. He wore a long gray-and-white fur coat and tall, black boots. His wavy brown hair fell past his collar. The man smiled at Vlad, and his ice blue eyes twinkled.

Otis stepped forward and embraced the man. "Vikas. It's good to see you again, old friend."

Vikas squeezed Otis in a hug before patting him solidly on the back. "It is always a pleasure to see you, my friend." His eyes returned to Vlad. "So this is Tomas's son."

For a moment, Vlad thought he saw within his gaze an eager glint. Removing his leather gloves, Vikas took Vlad's hand in his and shook. His grip was rough, his skin cool. "It will be a great honor to teach you. Tomas is my dearest friend . . . next to Otis, of course."

Vlad smiled in relief. He'd half expected Vikas to look down his nose at him for only being half-vampire, but he could tell by Vikas's eyes that this was a kind soul, and that he'd cared very much for Vlad's father. "It's nice to meet you. Otis says you're the oldest vampire he knows."

Vikas smiled warmly. "He speaks the truth, young one. But he forgets that I am also the best-looking, most charming, and—"

"Humble. You forgot humble." Otis was wearing a smirk.

Vikas laughed and turned to Vlad. "What is your name, boy?"

"Vlad."

Vikas nodded, his eyes suddenly troubled. "A good Russian name."

Vlad shrugged. "Well, it's actually Vladimir."

"Still a good, strong Russian name. It means 'to rule with peace.'" Vikas smiled, but his smile was forced. "You must be hungry from your journey. Come. We will feast and you will tell me how Tomas has been these past fifteen years." He patted Vlad roughly on the back and strode forward, toward the largest cabin nestled in the valley below.

Otis and Vlad exchanged glances and followed.

11
VIKAS

INSIDE THE CABIN, it sounded like a party was going on. Vikas stepped up to the large wooden door. To Vlad's amazement, the door lacked a knob. However, an intricate glyph was carved into the wood at its center. Vikas touched it, eliciting a cool glow from the strange symbol. Vlad wished that he could see Vikas's eyes from where he was standing, to note whether his eyes changed colors the way that Vlad's did whenever he touched a glyph, but it was impossible to tell from where he was standing.

The door swung open and Vikas stepped inside. Otis followed. Voices rose in greeting. But when Vlad stepped in after his uncle, every eye turned on him, and the room fell shockingly silent.

Vikas waved to the others to continue their feast. Almost immediately, the room returned to its previously chatter-filled state.

But that feeling—that creepy, crawly, "everyone is watching me" feeling stuck hard in Vlad's chest.

At one end of the long plank table in the center of the room was a high-back chair. Along the sides were groupings of wooden benches and smaller, semicircular chairs. Vikas took the large seat at the head of the table and directed Vlad and Otis to sit on either side of him. After they did so, Vikas looked at Vlad. "Do you enjoy meat?"

Vlad shifted his feet and glanced about the room. If these people were vampires, they sure didn't act like it. A rotund man at the table was reaching for a chicken leg, and across the table a woman was chewing thoughtfully on some ham. Vlad nearly retched at the idea of eating meat—especially cooked meat. He shook his head. "Not really."

"A blood drinker only? You were well bred." Vikas's lips wore the hint of a smile. He patted a rough hand on Vlad's shoulder. A young man, youngest of the crowd next to Vlad, rushed over and thrust a pewter goblet into Vlad's hands. It was full to the brim with what looked and smelled like blood. He filled Otis's glass and then Vikas's, inciting a grateful nod from Vikas. "*Spasibo*, Tristian."

Vlad glanced at Otis, who nodded. He put the cup to his lips and sipped. The liquid was warm and spiced. It was clearly blood—O positive, Vlad was sure—but behind that tangy flavor was another, spicier taste. Herbs came to mind, like ginger or maybe curry.

Otis wasn't drinking. Instead, he was staring into his goblet, as if there he would find the words to tell Vikas that their friend, Vlad's father, was dead. When he looked up, it seemed he'd lost his courage. "I'm grateful you've agreed to instruct the boy, Vikas. It means worlds to both of us. I know Tomas would be bursting with gratitude if he were here to see it."

"It is my honor to teach the boy, as I taught both his father and his uncle the ways of Elysia." Vikas smiled and emptied his goblet. He held it out to Tristian, who refilled it without hesitation. "So, Vladimir, what think you of Russia so far?"

Vlad tried to think of a compliment. It wasn't hard. The countryside he'd seen by dogsled was breathtaking. But it sounded like such a cop-out to say Vikas's homeland was beautiful. Vlad cleared his throat and let his second thought slip out of his mouth. "It's cold here."

All eyes around the table were locked on him again. At the same moment, each of the gathered vampires burst into hearty laughter. Vikas followed suit.

Vlad breathed a small sigh of relief.

That strange feeling that they were all still watching him lessened . . . but not by much.

Vikas relaxed back in his seat. "True, she may be a cold woman, our mother Russia, but her beauty is incomparable, and her loyalty unchallenged. Siberia is one of the great untouched places in the world."

They ate and drank for over an hour—Otis even convinced Vlad to give the beef Stroganov a try. He hated it and immediately spit the cooked meat and sauce into his napkin, but at least he tried it. After he did, Vikas gestured for Tristian to refill Vlad's glass. "So tell me, Mahlyenki Dyavol, how my dear friend Tomas is fairing. I have missed his company greatly."

Vlad paused at the strange name and exchanged glances with Otis. Otis's eyes shimmered, and Vlad cleared his throat. It had to be said. "I'm sorry to be the one to tell you, Vikas. But . . . my parents died four years ago in a house fire."

The crowd grew grimly silent. Stunned faces turned to look at Vlad. One vampire dropped his chicken leg back onto his plate. Goblets of bloodwine slowly found their way back to the table.

Vikas slumped back in his chair, and with terrible, disbelieving pain in his eyes, he looked at Otis. "Is this true? Tomas is dead?"

At his nod, Vikas dropped his eyes. For a moment it seemed the revelry had ended, but then Vikas raised his goblet high and called out, "To our fallen comrade!"

Every glass was raised and every voice cried out, "To our fallen comrade!" over and over again. Vlad's eyes misted over. He had no idea his dad had been so beloved.

Or that his dad had ever been to Siberia.

At the far end of the table, a group of vampires began to sing in thick Russian accents. They swayed back and forth as their voices rose and fell. Vlad smiled at them and listened, wondering what exactly they were singing. Otis leaned closer and explained, "They sing a tribute to your father—a song of brotherhood and valor. It's an old tune that Tomas used to sing whenever he would return triumphant from a hunt during the Middle Ages, when so much human blood was tainted by the Black Death. Many vampires survived those dark times due to your father's skill."

Vlad looked back at Vikas, who seemed to be expecting his glance. "You saw this? This fire?"

Vlad nodded slowly and returned his goblet to the table. Suddenly, he wasn't hungry anymore.

"Tomorrow, we will hold a funeral in your father's honor— a blissfully rare occasion for vampirekind." Vikas took the pitcher from Tristian and refilled Vlad's glass himself before thrusting the goblet back into his hands. "But today, right now, we will drink to your father's memory, and you will tell me the details of this horrific event, Mahlyenki Dyavol. No vampire should suffer such a tragic loss alone. We are family. And we shall shed tears for Tomas as one."

Hot tears rolled from Vlad's eyes and coated his cheeks. When he lifted his gaze to Vikas, he saw that Vikas was crying, too. Vlad said, "It was my fault."

Otis and Vikas exchanged looks. Otis shook his head. Vikas settled back in his chair. "Tell me what happened."

Vlad's breath shook, but once he began speaking, the words poured out of him—and in his mind's eye, he could see the day so clearly, as if it were just now happening to him. "I woke up early that morning and snuck into their bedroom to turn off their alarms. They never got to sleep in, y'know? So I thought I'd be nice and get myself ready for school, let them rest late. If I hadn't done that . . . if I hadn't turned off their alarms, they wouldn't have been sleeping when the fire started."

Otis sat stone-faced, all color gone from his lips. Vikas gestured to Vlad's glass, and Vlad drank. "Were you there when it began?"

"No. I was at school. The office sent a girl down to get me. I asked her if I was in trouble. She said, 'No, your house is on fire.' Just like that. No empathy. No pity. Just 'your house is on fire,' like it happens every day." Vlad's tears lessened in momentary anger. He furrowed his brow and shook his head. After a moment, he spoke again, but this time his voice was lower, as if speaking these things aloud might awaken something ugly within him. "I ran home after that. Smoke was pouring out of the windows of their bedroom. A fire truck was there, police cars, an ambulance,

I think. It's all a blur now. I ran past them all just to get upstairs. I had to find Mom and Dad, make sure they were okay. But when I reached the bedroom . . ."

Vlad burst into tears. He didn't fight them, couldn't fight them. His mom and dad were dead. Dead and gone and never, ever coming back. Worse yet, he didn't know for certain if it was an accident that took them or somebody's sick idea of justice.

He wiped his eyes with his sleeve and continued, though his voice broke several times. "They were on the bed, already gone. And when I saw them, I felt more alone than I'd ever felt."

He looked to Otis, who had his face buried in his hands. It was the first time Vlad had revealed any details of the accident to anyone but Henry. "I don't remember how exactly, but I ended up at Nelly's house, and I've been there ever since."

Vikas sat quietly for a long time, and when his tears dried, he looked pointedly at Vlad. "You are not alone, Vladimir. You are never alone in this world. You are a member of Elysia. And had Tomas a choice, he'd have raised you among your own kind. But these laws . . . they must be changed."

Otis dried his eyes on a linen napkin, as if in desperate need of a subject change—something Vlad certainly didn't object to. Otis leaned forward with his elbows on the table. "Have you heard anything from the Stokerton council?"

Vikas shook his head slowly. "Nothing but lies, my friend. They insist you are a criminal. What did the council in London have to say about your plight?"

Otis's shoulders slumped some as he sighed. "Only that upon confirmation from Stokerton I would be regarded as a fugitive, and they would be forced to take me into cus- tody immediately to be charged with assisting in an attack on the Stokerton council president, aiding and abetting a known fugitive, and revealing my true identity to three humans."

"The fugitive is Tomas?" One of Vikas's eyebrow rose in a pointed arch. He did not look pleased.

Otis released a sigh. "They refuse to believe that he is dead."

Vlad bit his bottom lip thoughtfully. "What if I tell them what I saw? Then they'd have to believe it."

Otis pursed his lips and shook his head once, his stern eyes locked on Vlad. "I don't want you anywhere near those councils until this matter is cleared up."

Vlad sank down in his chair, clutching his half-empty goblet to his chest. "I'm just trying to help."

Otis managed a smile then, and his features softened. "Don't worry, Vlad. I'm in good hands here with Vikas, and I have friends all over the world who are willing to help me."

"Vampire friends?"

"Of course."

Vlad furrowed his brow in confusion. "Wait a minute. You only revealed to two humans that you're a vampire—Nelly and Henry."

"I also revealed it to you. Remember, Vladimir, so long as you carry the Lucis, all of Elysia insists that you are human—even though they know that is not the case. They would rather insist on that than admit that they are incapable of bringing a child to justice, due to the terrible possibility that you may be what they fear you to be. Pride is a terrible weakness to have." Otis released a sigh and reached for his glass. "Of course, should they find a way to take the Lucis from you . . . you'll be in as much trouble as I am."

Vikas shook his head. "If not more. He did take D'Ablo's life. His very existence, in fact, is an abomination in the eyes of their ridiculous laws."

Vlad raised an eyebrow. "Are the laws different here in Siberia?"

"Here we live as free men. We come and go as we please, and only the most heinous crimes are tended to by council."

Otis's voice had grown gruff. "Some might not think their laws ridiculous, Vikas. I could have stopped Vlad from taking D'Ablo's life but didn't. I knew of Tomas and Mellina's love affair but assisted in their escape by not telling anyone. And I did reveal my true nature to humans, that I won't deny. My quibble is not whether or not I did these things, but whether or not I did them for the right reason."

Vikas's eyes met with Otis's. "The majority of Elysia says that you were wrong."

"And perhaps they are right. If I am, I will face justice." Otis nodded at his possible fate, as if the torturous punishments Vlad had read about in the *Encyclopedia Vampyrica* were nothing at all to endure.

Vlad stared in fascination.

Vikas shook his head in disgust. "You have a skewed view of the world, Otis. Tomas would never have wanted—"

Otis slammed his goblet on the table. "Tomas DIED believing in those laws! He was the Stokerton council vice president, Vikas. Or have you forgotten?"

The room grew eerily silent then. Vlad squirmed in his seat.

Otis closed his eyes briefly and opened them again, once more calm. He flashed Vlad an apologetic glance. Without needing telepathy, Vlad could tell that his recollection of the day he'd found his parents dead had shaken Otis's nerves. Why else would he snap like that?

After a moment, Vikas spoke. His voice was soft and calming. "I have not forgotten. Nor have I forgotten how deeply you questioned that choice when he made it. But we all make mistakes. Tomas chose to enforce unjust laws. I chose to judge you for your past actions in front of your nephew. And you have always supported your brother, even when he was wrong. There is no crime in that. However, you've also spilled your bloodwine, and that, my friend, is a crime."

The corner of his mouth rose in a smirk, and soon, Otis's followed.

Relieved that the sudden, strange tension had dissipated, Vlad cleared his throat. "So there are three councils altogether?"

Otis sopped up the spilled bloodwine with a rag and nodded his thanks to Tristian as his mug was refilled. "Nine, actually. Stokerton, London, Siberia, Beijing, Paris, Athens, Edinburgh, Mexico City, and Cairo. And so far, I'm wanted by all but London and Siberia."

"What happens if you get caught?" Vlad was sure he didn't want to know the answer but felt obliged to ask. The *Encyclopedia Vampyrica* had listed several horrific punishments for vampires who broke the laws of Elysia, and he couldn't stomach the idea of Otis enduring any of them.

As if Otis knew what he was thinking, he shook his head slowly.

Vikas shook his head as well and gestured for Tristian to refill his glass. "If you do not mind, I've had enough talk of death for the evening."

Otis placed a hand on Vikas's shoulder and squeezed. They exchanged glances quietly, and it dawned on Vlad that they were likely carrying on a conversation he couldn't hear. After a moment, Vikas laughed warmly and looked back to Vlad. "Did your father ever mention me, Vladimir?"

Vlad shook his head. His dad hadn't even mentioned that he'd had a brother, let alone that there was an entire world of vampires out there. It bugged Vlad. After all, what could he have gained by keeping Elysia secret? Still, he reminded himself, his dad had fled Elysia and had likely done so for what he considered to be very good reasons. "He didn't really talk about his life before meeting Mom. Were you close?"

"Have you never mentioned me to this boy?" Vikas flashed an astounded glance at Otis, who stammered. Vikas looked back at Vlad with a bemused twinkle in his eye. "Close, yes. I was made into a vampire many years before your father and uncle, but we nevertheless shared a kinship from the day we met. It was immediate, as if we'd been friends all along. The man who made Otis had also made Tomas—they were brothers. And I was their grateful tagalong. For a time, they even shared my home here. Together we found more trouble and shared more laughter than any friends I have ever known."

Otis swallowed a mouthful of the sweet liquid. "I'm sorry, Vikas. I should have told him more about you."

"No need for apologies, my friend. If there is one subject I enjoy sharing tales about, it is of the three of us." Vikas leaned closer to Vlad, as if energized by memories of the past. "Before young Vladimir returns to the Americas, we shall have a good, long chat about what troublemakers his father and uncle were in their younger years." He offered Otis a wink, and Otis smiled through a cringe.

For several more hours they ate, drank, and spoke of happier times.

Vlad watched the scene before him in fascination. He couldn't speak. He could only nod occasionally and marvel at the company he was keeping. These vampires were nothing like those in Stokerton. They'd welcomed him in like family.

Vlad leaned closer to Otis. "What is it that Vikas keeps calling me?"

Otis smiled. "Mahlyenki Dyavol."

"Yes, but what does it mean?"

Otis and Vikas exchanged glances. Both broke into bemused laughter. Otis raised his glass to Vlad with a drunken grin. "It means 'Little Devil.'"

After another bout of laughter, Vikas and Otis engaged in private conversation. They slipped easily from English to Russian and at one point into French. Vlad listened but didn't bother trying to figure out what they were saying. He couldn't help but wonder exactly why Vikas had given him such a weird nickname, but at the moment, he didn't feel like pressing the issue. Otis and Vikas were clearly enjoying their reunion, and he didn't really feel like distracting them from that. He reached out for his cup, his sleeve pulling up and revealing his mark. A thin, rather gray vampire across the table nodded to Vlad and smiled approvingly at the tattoo on Vlad's wrist. Vlad beamed, drank from his glass, and sank down in his chair, content to share space with his vampire brethren.

So this was Elysia.

As the night wore on, the room slowly cleared until only Vlad, Vikas, and Otis remained.

Otis placed his goblet on the table next to Vlad's. He looked happier than Vlad had ever seen him. "I owe you much gratitude for your hospitality, Vikas. I have not enjoyed the likes of Elysia in some time."

Vikas smiled, refilling Otis's goblet. "It is my pleasure. I hope that you will consider remaining on a permanent basis. I'm quite certain we can clear up the misunderstanding in Stokerton."

Otis's smile slipped. He shook his head. "No. I can't risk it. But thank you for offering."

Vlad stretched. Before he could form the words I'm tired on his lips, Vikas said, "Rest now, Mahlyenki Dyavol. Tomorrow we honor your father's memory, and the next day, we begin lessons on mind control and the finer points of telepathy."

With a yawn, Vlad followed Tristian to one of the spare bedrooms and collapsed into bed. His head had barely hit the pillow before his eyes were closed and he was sleeping peacefully.

12
HONORING TOMAS TOD

V LAD HEAVED THE LOG onto the pile and brushed the flakes of bark from his gloves. With little effort Otis tossed on two more—each twice as large as the one Vlad had struggled with, Vlad noticed with an exhausted sigh. As Otis turned back to the wood that Vikas had chopped to grab another two pieces, Vlad looked around the village with a curious crinkle in his brow. "Not many people here this morning. Where are they all?"

Otis dropped the new logs on the pile and smiled. "A large percentage of the Siberian council chooses not to rise during daylight hours, believing it to be against vampiric nature."

Vlad glanced over at Vikas, who had removed his shirt and was raising an ax over another large log. "But isn't Vikas their president?"

"Oh yes. And much beloved." Otis crossed his arms in front of him and leaned up against the pile of wood they'd created. It was already waist-high.

Vlad raised an eyebrow. "So shouldn't they follow his example?"

Otis chuckled. "If citizens followed their leaders' example throughout history, the human race would have died out centuries ago."

Vlad weighed this for a moment and then looked back at Vikas, who had paused to wipe his brow. "What do they think of him being out in the sun?"

"From what I've heard, they think his willingness to move about on human time borders on sacrilege. Nevertheless, when they travel to Novosibirsk every month for supplies, they are sure to purchase plenty of sunblock." Otis patted him on the shoulder and met his eyes. "Just because they disagree with him doesn't mean they love him any less, Vladimir."

Vikas dropped the axe and carried the remaining pieces of wood over to the pile. After setting them carefully on top, he patted the wood. "A good kindling for our funeral pyre."

Otis nodded, agreeing with his assessment.

Vlad blinked. "But doesn't a funeral pyre usually contain a . . . a . . ."

"A body? Yes." Vikas offered him a reassuring nod. "Normally the wood is set aflame at dusk and kept burning all through the night until the body is placed on the flames moments before dawn. Words are said, good-byes are given, honor is bestowed, and the living vampires retire inside just as the sun begins to rise. The body bursts into flames at dawn, when the sun's rays touch it, and it continues to burn until the next evening, when all that is left are ashes . . . and memories."

Vlad bit his bottom lip gently for a moment. "But my dad is buried back in Bathory."

"A defilement that we will one day correct, Mahlyenki Dyavol. Burying the dead is barbaric. It has no honor. Putting a body in a box as a keepsake for mortals to cling to long after everything that was that person is gone—it turns my stomach. Graveyards are for the living, not the dead." Vikas tore his eyes from the woodpile and lowered his head. "Pardon me, Vladimir. I don't mean to insult your heritage."

Vlad didn't speak. He couldn't. For a brief moment, he'd felt like he'd belonged somewhere, that he was simply another vampire. But the spell had been broken by Vikas's observation. He was just as much of a freak to vampires as he was to humans.

Aside from that, it was astounding to learn how drastically different vampire traditions were from the human traditions he'd grown up with. They really had little in common, apart from hunter and hunted, if you thought about it.

Vlad's stomach rumbled.

Vikas smiled. "I hunger as well. But hold your fast, Mahl-yenki Dyavol. We cannot eat until the dusk following your father's funeral. It is tradition. Tomas can no longer imbibe the essence of life, and so we, too, will not imbibe until his memory has been honored."

Vlad nodded in understanding. The sun had already begun its descent, and the sky was turning various shades of pink and gold. As it darkened, lights appeared in the windows of the cabins. It seemed the rest of the vampires were awake. Which meant Tomas's funeral was about to begin.

Vlad glanced at Otis, who was sitting somberly on the bench next to him. His uncle looked tired but proud, sad but grateful that this moment was being shared. Vlad could tell, because he felt the same. The vigil had lasted all night, just hours and hours of stoking the flames and of complete and total silence—both in voice and in telepathy. All of the gathered vampires focused quietly on one thing: their memories of Tomas Tod, Vlad's father.

At last, Vikas stood and moved to the center of the gathered crowd, near the crackling funeral pyre. Each vampire looked up at him then, as if coaxed by a thought. Then Vlad heard Vikas's voice in his head, too. It was deep and thickly accented, warm and comforting, just like his spoken voice. He said, "We begin."

Suddenly, Vlad's weary body and mourning mind relaxed, and he settled back on the bench in awe of the towering flames.

Once Vikas had their attention, he spoke aloud. "Tomas Tod was many things. Friend, family . . ." He gestured to Vlad with a nod. "Even father. But before all of those things, he was a vampire. The greatest, in fact, that I have ever known in all my nine hundred and ninety-eight years."

Vlad suppressed a gasp. Vikas looked no older than thirty-five, had not a single strand of gray in his hair, and yet here he was, proclaiming to be just two years short of a millennium. Vlad made a mental note to ask Otis later what the oldest vampire had lived to be.

Vikas glanced to the fire and took a shuddered breath, fighting tears that had been threatening to fall since he heard the news of Tomas's death. "Tonight we honor him in death as he honored us in life. And as Tomas embraced his son, Vladimir, so shall we embrace him as a brother, a vampire, a son. As for Tomas's chosen bride . . ."

Several vampires shifted uncomfortably. One stood to leave, and then, at Vikas's glance, he sat once more. Vikas looked at Vlad and nodded. "Mellina stood by Tomas's side when none of us could, during the extended period he spent without the comfort of Elysia, and also during his most terrible and unexpected demise. We owe her, young Vladimir's mother, great respect. And tonight, we honor her as we honor her husband, our brother.

"Tomas was but a fledgling vampire when first he was brought into my teaching. Wise beyond his years, eager to learn, with an amazing—and somewhat distracting—sense of humor. It was that same day that he and Otis would meet, and through them both, I would learn the true value of friendship." Vikas's smile grew and his eyes glistened. "Tomas was a gifted student, particularly in the skill of manipulating the minds of others. I recall fondly our first visit to Moscow together. I'd been teaching Tomas for just two weeks. To my amazement, he manipulated several dozen tourists to dance around a grand fountain there. And when the humans sent their police to break up the impromptu celebration, Tomas had them join in with grand pirouettes. It was quite the sight."

Despite the solemnity of the occasion, several vampires laughed aloud. Vikas dried his eyes, and once the laughter ceased, he spoke again. "It was troubling for many of us to learn that Tomas had abandoned Elysia for the love of a human. But we must remember that Tomas was not one to follow in the footsteps of others, but rather seek out fresh ground and make his own way. He was a criminal, yes, but he was also a pioneer, a great man, and one who more vampires should seek to emulate."

Vikas looked from vampire to vampire until each had met his gaze and understood the seriousness of what he was about to say. Vlad swallowed his tears and listened.

"A part of me—a part of us—has died. Let us never forget that."

Vikas stared into the flames for a moment in what looked like silent prayer, then glanced up at the lightening sky and released his tears. One by one, each vampire stood in silence near the flames before turning away and moving indoors. Otis gestured to the pyre with a nod. Vlad stood and followed, but once they were at the fireside, he didn't know what he was expected to do.

"It is customary to say good-bye, but none can ask that of you, just as none can ask that of Vikas or me." Otis met Vlad's eyes and squeezed his shoulder.

"Just tell him whatever you would if he were listening. He is, you know. From wherever we go after life, Tomas is listening." Otis choked back more tears. He and Vikas turned and made their way slowly to the largest cabin, leaving Vlad alone at the pyre.

Vlad stood there for several minutes. The sun was breaking over the horizon. If he was going to at least try to keep with vampire tradition, he'd better think of something to say soon. But what could he say to his dad that he hadn't said aloud to Tomas's picture every night for four years now?

He cleared his throat and looked into the flames. "I miss you, Dad. Otis is teaching me a lot. And Vikas is about to. I hope . . . I hope that I make you proud. I'm trying."

He turned from the fire and took one step before he paused and whispered into the chilly air. "And don't worry, Dad. I'll never say good-bye. Otis is right. No one can ask that of me. Ever."

Vlad quickened his pace and hurried into the largest cabin. The door had just closed behind him when the sunlight hit the pyre.

13
Mind Control

Vlad opened the door to find Vikas waiting. "Come, Vladimir. It is time to learn."

Blinking back tears, Vlad said, "So, the funeral is over?"

Vikas nodded. "For the most part. We will continue our fast until nightfall and then feast. Only then is the funeral officially at an end. Mind you, you may not have much luck with telepathy or mind control while you hunger, but we must try. There isn't much time before you return to the Americas."

"Actually," Vlad began timidly, "I find it easier to read minds when I'm hungry."

Vikas eyed him for a moment with what looked to Vlad like disbelief. After several seconds, he took a breath and released it in a sigh. "Perhaps I will not be the only teacher this week. Are you ready to begin?"

Vlad shifted his weight from one foot to the other. "What do I do?"

"You come with me. We want no distractions." He crossed the room to another door, and they moved outside the other end of the cabin. As they moved down the steps and began crossing the snow toward another cabin, Vikas explained, "This place that I am taking you, it is a room without windows, without light, and so well insulated that it is also without external noise. You may panic at first, but hold your will. The idea is to remove any external influences so that you may tap into your deepest telepathic powers."

Vlad swallowed the lump in his throat, which hadn't been there a moment before. "Will you go in with me?"

Vikas cast him a reassuring glance. "Yes. Yes, of course."

A small cabin was ahead of them. True to Vikas's words, it had no windows and only one door. With a deep breath for bravery, Vlad followed Vikas up the steps and inside. The light from outside drew a long line along the floor. Vlad could see two stools in the middle of the room; that was all there was. When Vikas closed the door, Vlad felt as if he might never see that light again. He took several calming breaths before looking around. It was useless—the room was pitch-black. The only sound was Vlad's breathing and Vikas's slow, steady heartbeat.

"Now, Mahlyenki Dyavol, I want you to focus on your heart, on the blood pumping through your veins, on the air as it enters and exits your lungs. Feel the life within you, the energies pouring out of you."

Vlad did as he was instructed. At first, he closed his eyes, but once he realized what a ridiculous and futile action that was, he opened them wide to the dark room. His heartbeat had slowed some, not as calm as Vikas's, but calmer than it had been. His blood rushed through his veins, and his breaths were deep and even.

Vikas's voice was soft and coaxing. "Good. Very good. Now push gently with your mind into mine. What am I thinking at this moment?"

"You're thinking"—Vlad choked back tears—"you're thinking about how much I look like my dad."

"Very good, Vladimir. Now I want you to focus on Otis. Where is he? What is he doing, thinking? How does he feel? Push hard if you have to and don't be disappointed if you can't reach him. Distance is something that many vampires struggle with."

Vlad took a deep breath and pictured Otis's face in his mind. He thought of blood and how empty his stomach was, how delicious a nice warm blood bag would be right about now. Then he pushed with his mind.

Otis removed his gloves with shaking fingers. He hadn't realized how difficult it would be to see Vlad go through the funeral festivities. The entire time, he could feel pain emanating from his nephew but could do nothing to stop it. Vikas was teaching the boy already, and Otis couldn't help but wonder what might be unearthed in the training room. Whatever happened, it would be a glimpse of how powerful Vlad might one day become. It was in this room that a vampire had no distractions from his powers, so it was there that he could experience a taste of what practice and experience might lead to. Many a vampire had left the room disappointed and feeling weak. Otis recalled leaving the room full of hope. He'd demonstrated skill beyond his level of understanding and hoped that much for Vlad. But there was no telling, not with his mother's human blood tainting his veins. He might leave with the knowledge that he would never get past the basics. A disappointment for them both.

Otis rested his head in his hands. But what if the prophecy were right? What if Vladimir was the Pravus?

Otis sat up suddenly. In his mind, he felt a curious prickling, almost as if someone was poking around in there. . . .

Vlad pulled out of Otis's thoughts with a gasp.

Vikas's tone sounded slightly anxious. "You saw something. This surprised you. Tell me how it is that you read minds. Do you see the words written? Hear them?"

Vlad cleared his throat. "Neither. I kind of become the person. I see and hear and feel and think along with them."

Vikas was quiet for a long time. Vlad was about to ask if something was wrong, when he finally spoke. Vlad thought he detected a note of excitement and surprise in his tone. "You mentioned your drudge last evening. Where is he?"

"Henry? He's back in Bathory." Vlad strained but couldn't recall having brought up Henry at all the night before. "Why?"

"Reach him with your mind." Vikas's voice was calm again, but it felt to Vlad as if Vikas was trying hard to keep it so.

"That's halfway around the world. I don't think I can—"

"Try. The chamber removes the difficulties you encounter in your normal routine. In here, you may reach people you had little or no success at reaching outside."

Vlad sighed and relaxed his muscles. He focused on Henry and pushed.

Henry looked over at Joss. He had no idea what his cousin was doing, but it certainly wasn't winning. He pushed the turbo button, slashed Joss's android to pieces, and raised his arms triumphantly above his head. There was no doubt about it, Joss was even worse at video games than Vlad.

But at least Vlad was a challenge at times.

Vlad pulled out of Henry's mind with a smirk and made a mental note to play against Joss more. If nothing else, it might be good for his self-esteem.

"Excellent. You are indeed skilled, Mahlyenki Dyavol." Vikas took a deep breath. "Now we move on to mind control. I want you to push into Otis's mind again. But this time, I want you to insert an action into his thought process. Take over control gently, so that he is completely unaware, and make him scratch his forehead."

Vlad shifted his feet but he didn't push into Otis's mind. It felt weird, the idea of controlling Otis. Henry was one thing, but this was his uncle.

"Is something wrong?"

"No. I just . . ." Vlad cleared his throat and tried impossibly to look at Vikas in the darkness. "If you don't mind, I'd rather focus on—"

"Vladimir, this is an important part of your lessons. You must learn to control the minds of others. Your drudge will be much easier to control. After that, those whom you care little or nothing for. The most difficult to control are those closest to you, whom you feel great affection for. This is a mental block that most vampires cannot break. But you have the potential to become as great a vampire as I have ever seen. More powerful than your father. Indeed, perhaps even more powerful than myself. But you must—"

"None of that matters to me." Vlad's voice shook slightly. He really didn't want to disappoint Vikas, but this was something he wasn't willing to budge on. If controlling Henry made him feel even slightly guilty, controlling his uncle would make him feel entirely sick.

Vikas lowered his voice so that Vlad had to strain in order to hear him. "But it should. So few vampires have your potential. I had thought your mother's blood would dilute your abilities, but I was wrong. You could be a great vampire, Vladimir. But you must trust me."

Vlad closed his eyes and opened them again. He'd adjusted to the darkness but had grown tired of seeing it. "I'm sorry, Vikas. I just . . . can't do what you want me to."

"Enough. If I must be stern with you, I will. See Otis in your mind. He's sitting at the table alone, his forehead resting in his left hand."

"Stop it. I won't."

"Just a nudge. Just a small movement. A scratch."

"NO!" Vlad pushed hard into Vikas's mind.

Vikas stumbled back, knocking his stool to the floor. The boy was strong, of that there was no doubt . . . but he was tired, far from home, and clearly didn't want to learn how to control the actions of others, least of all his uncle. It was time to break for the day.

Vlad pulled out of Vikas's thoughts.

"It is time to break for the day, Vladimir."

Vlad hadn't wanted to control him, but he'd had little choice.

Vikas opened the door, and the light poured in, welcoming them outside. They'd just moved down the steps when Vikas paused. "That was uncalled for, Mahlyenki Dyavol. There was no need to control my mind."

Vlad shook his head. He should have felt guilty but didn't. "But you wouldn't listen to reason."

After a moment, Vikas smiled warmly. "Ah, so perhaps now you see why this is such a necessary skill to develop."

Vlad chewed his bottom lip thoughtfully. Vikas had a point.

The door to the largest cabin opened, and Otis stepped outside. There was an eager glint in his eye. "How'd it go?"

Vikas kept his voice low, but his excitement leaked through. "You were right about him, Otis. Your nephew is enormously talented. He even managed to end his lessons early with mind control."

Otis's jaw dropped.

Vlad was about to apologize when his uncle and Vikas burst into laughter. Vikas patted him on the shoulder. "Come. We'll warm ourselves by the hearth until the feast begins."

Vikas climbed the steps to the cabin and touched the glyph, opening the door. Vlad started to follow, but Otis stopped him with a gentle hand to the chest. Otis leaned closer and whispered into Vlad's ear, "If I ever find you lurking about in my thoughts again, Vlad, I will be most displeased. You stay out of my mind, and I'll stay out of yours. Agreed?"

Vlad flushed at all the things he'd rather his uncle didn't know about him, like his late-night trips to the belfry, and nodded. "Agreed."

They made their way inside, and Vlad spent the better part of the day sitting in front of the hearth in a big, cushy chair, listening as Otis and Vikas recounted tales of their adventures. They spoke often of Tomas, and occasionally, one of the other vampires would join them to exchange a tale of Tomas's heroics or something humorous that had once happened to them while in Tomas's presence. At the end of yet another tale, Otis chuckled. "I told Tomas not to frighten Vikas like that, but in the end I was rather hoping he would."

Vikas laughed loudly. "You were terrible guests that summer, and lucky that I hold no grudges."

At one point, Vlad noticed that it seemed all of the vampires of Siberia were awake and moving about. He was about to whisper to Otis to ask why they stayed awake during this day when he realized that the answer was obvious: it was their day to honor Tomas, and as Tomas no longer slept, so they would remain awake until the feast had ended.

By the time the sun disappeared below the horizon, Vlad had almost forgotten his immense and demanding hunger.

Almost.

The door opened, and every person in the room, but for Otis, Vikas, Tristian, and Vlad, filed outside in a rush. At Vlad's raised eyebrow, Vikas smiled. "So the feast begins."

Vlad furrowed his brow in confusion. "But there's plenty of bloodwine here. Where are they going?"

Otis and Vikas exchanged glances before Otis regarded Vlad with a somber gaze. He spoke in a gentle tone. "They go to feast from the source, Vladimir. Vikas and I will feast here with you as a courtesy."

Vlad's stomach twisted. People. They were going to feed on people. The idea shouldn't have nauseated him, but it did. He threw a glance across the room at Tristian, who was gathering goblets and a pitcher of bloodwine. "What about Tristian? Will he feed on people tonight, too?"

Vikas sat back in his seat, surprised. "My apologies for not explaining earlier, Mahlyenki Dyavol, but Tristian is no vampire."

Vlad sat forward slowly, confused.

"He is my faithful drudge and has been so for ten years now, since he was just your age."

Vlad watched Tristian carry the beginnings of their feast toward them and shook his head slowly. He'd had no idea this man was anything but a vampire—even his mannerisms seemed similar to theirs. "How long will he be your drudge?"

Vikas smiled warmly at Vlad, but, Vlad noticed, he barely cast a glance at Tristian. "All his mortal life."

Vlad took a mouthful of bloodwine, rolling the mixture over his tongue and relishing its tangy taste and silken texture. He glanced from Tristian back to Vikas. "Henry's a good drudge. I just wish he had my back a little more. He's pretty absent when it comes to these jerks at school knocking me around."

Vikas smiled. "It is not a drudge's place to protect a vampire, Vladimir. Quite the opposite, actually. It is theirs only to watch over you as you sleep, if you slept during the day, and to recommend possible food sources, as well as run errands for you. No more. We vampires must defend ourselves."

Vlad sighed. Great. Now not only was he less protected than he thought he was but he was also on his own when it came to bullies. He tried to picture himself and Henry existing in the same way as Vikas and Tristian, and couldn't. But one thing rang clear for him. If there ever came a time when Henry didn't want to be his drudge, Vlad would give him his freedom that moment and without question . . . if he could.

Vlad turned to his uncle with a surge of curiosity. "Otis, if all a vampire has to do to create a drudge is bite them, why isn't the world overrun with drudges?"

Vikas and Otis exchanged glances before Otis spoke. "Most humans do not survive our bites, Vladimir. We often kill to be kind, to end what would be a life of slavery for them before it has begun."

Vikas's jaw grew tight. "Do not gloss over the larger truth, my friend. Most vampires kill out of pleasure, not pity."

Vlad mulled this over for a bit, then asked, "So why don't drudges turn into vampires?"

Otis snapped his eyes back to Vlad, as if breaking off a silent conversation with Vikas. When he spoke, his voice was soft, kind. "A vampire infuses his essence with his intended creation—this is sometimes done with a blood exchange, but can be carried on in many ways. However, as with setting glyphs—something you'll learn more about later—the vampire's intent is key."

Vlad nodded. Intent made a lot of sense.

Vlad was awakened by the sound of someone slamming their fist down on a table. He sat up in bed and listened. Through the door drifted Otis's voice, shaking with anger. "He is not what gossip deems him to be!"

Vikas's voice, calm but certain, followed. "And what if he is? What if Vladimir Tod is the Pravus?"

A long, silent moment went by.

Finally, Otis spoke again, but this time, his voice was broken by tears. "I am at a loss for words."

"Then allow me to speak. How did Vladimir obtain the Lucis? That is an enormous amount of power for a young boy to wield."

Otis exhaled a long sigh. "Tomas stole it from the Stokerton council. I imagine he'd wanted to protect Vlad from their vengeance—much good it has done."

"Vladimir is safe, so perhaps Tomas's thievery was wise after all." It sounded like Vikas refilled his goblet, and after several swallows, he continued. "It frightens you that he carries the Lucis with him?"

"Of course. But it frightens me more what might happen should he lose it." Otis's tone changed then, as if his utterance had surprised even him. "As you said, it's an enormous amount of power for a young boy."

Vikas's words quieted some. "Who could imagine Dom Augustine Calmet, kindest soul to ever enter Elysia, lover of humankind, builder of a bridge between our worlds, would be the creator of such a monstrous weapon?"

Vlad could hear his uncle pacing, as if growing increasingly impatient with their conversation. "He thought it was time for vampires to pass on from this world, that humans were fit to be the dominant species on Earth."

A small laugh from Vikas. "The fool."

"At least he knew where his loyalties lay."

"You question my loyalty?"

"I only question your reasons for not assisting me." A pause from Otis. "Come to Bathory. Watch over Vladimir in my absence. You can keep him safe. The Stokerton council wouldn't dare—"

"Let the boy stay here, then."

"I can't. His guardian would be heartbroken."

"Just as I would be heartbroken to abandon my post to act as nursemaid for a child who hardly needs one." It sounded like Vikas was pouring more bloodwine. He sighed and said, "You are troubled, Otis. And with good reason—running from Elysia has proven quite taxing on your soul. It has affected your reasoning."

Then, just as suddenly as the pacing had begun, it stopped. "Don't do this for me, then. Do it for Tomas, for our brother, our friend. Do it so that his memory will not perish along with his son. Protect him, Vikas. Protect Vlad."

Vikas spoke slowly, as if he wanted to be sure Otis understood his every word. "You ask too much, my friend."

Another moment of silence, followed by hurried footsteps and the slamming of a door—so loud that Vlad's heart jumped into his throat.

Vlad shivered, slipped out of bed, and closed the door behind him.

The fire was still crackling in the immense fireplace, filling the main room with a warm glow. Vlad moved toward it, rubbing his hands over the goose bumps on his arms. Vikas was seated in the chair facing the fire, watching the flames with intense focus. Vlad took the chair across from him. They were the only two in the room—something that both intrigued and comforted Vlad.

Heavy drapes covered the windows, but Vlad could see moonlight peeking into the room where the curtains met.

Vikas held up a pitcher of bloodwine. Vlad nodded and grabbed a goblet from the nearby table. Vikas filled it to the brim, and they settled back in their chairs with their drinks.

Vikas watched the flames in silence.

Vlad mulled over how to begin, what to say, but everything he thought of sounded like he'd be dancing around what he really wanted to talk about. After several minutes, he met Vikas's eyes. "I heard you arguing."

Vikas nodded, but he did not speak. Nor did he seem surprised.

Vlad cleared his throat. "You called me something."

"Does it bother you to be called Little Devil? I apologize."

"No, it's not that." Vlad looked into his goblet. "You called me the Pravus. What does that mean?"

Vikas's eyes were careful. He looked over Vlad's shoulder to the door Otis had slammed on his way out and then back at Vlad. "The story of the Pravus is an ancient one. Your uncle has not shared this tale with you?"

Vlad shook his head and took another drink. The spiced blood sent a delicious warmth through his body.

Vikas drained his glass and refilled it. He glanced over Vlad's shoulder again, before looking at Vlad with something that resembled determination in his eyes. "Long ago, when my grandfather was young . . . now mind you, Mahlyenki Dyavol, that my grandfather—that is to say the man who made my creator, my father, into a vampire—is now well over two thousand years old . . . but back then, when the wounds of his creation had barely had time to heal, an ancient prophecy was unearthed. It was probably the most important prophecy ever discovered for vampirekind. It told of a vampire of unique origin. One who was born, not made."

Something wet dripped onto Vlad's jeans. He looked down and cursed under his breath at the bloodwine he'd spilled. He hadn't even noticed he'd been leaning forward on the edge of his seat. He sat the glass down and relaxed back in his chair.

Vikas handed him a handkerchief and continued as Vlad dabbed at the stain. "The prophecy stated that a great and powerful vampire would one day come into our midst. One that laws would be broken to create. One who would be born of a human mother. He would have no sensitivity to sunlight, he would be able to manipulate the minds of most living creatures, and, it said, that he could not be killed by any means known to vampire or humankind. Injured, yes. But not killed. This man is the Pravus."

Vikas drained his glass and sat it beside Vlad's. "It is the belief of many in Elysia that the Pravus has come. And I know of only one vampire who has been born, Vladimir."

Vlad's eyes grew wide. His heart thumped hard against his insides, then settled into a quiet, steady beat. "Me."

"Not everyone believes that you are. In fact, a much larger group believes that you are not, and that the so-called prophecy is but a fairy tale. But there's more." Vikas stood and stepped closer to the fire. He placed one elbow on the mantel and propped his chin on his open hand, then tilted his head some so that he was looking at Vlad once again. "It is what I am about to share with you that steals peaceful sleep away from many of our brethren, Mahlyenki Dyavol, no matter what they believe about you."

Vikas turned to face Vlad. His shadow flickered against the wall to his right. His voice was gruff, as if the subject could easily bring even a man of his power to tears. He held Vlad's gaze. "It is prophesied that the Pravus will come to rule over all of vampirekind and that he will enslave the entire human race."

Vlad's jaw dropped.

Vikas nodded, as if to tell him that yes, it was true—even though Vlad hadn't offered otherwise.

The tattoo on the inside of Vlad's left wrist glowed brightly. He shook his head again, hardly able to comprehend what he was hearing. "I'm not the Pravus. Even if the prophecy is right and there will be some guy born someday like that . . . it's not me. I'm not him."

"Are you so sure?"

Vlad dropped his eyes. He wasn't sure of anything, really, but he was pretty sure he wasn't going to enslave the human race. After all, that would include Henry—and he had yet to beat him at *Race to Armageddon*, let alone its sequel. "Do you think I'm this human-enslaving, vampire-ruling monster?"

"Not a monster, a walking myth . . . and it is not important what I think."

Vlad took that as a yes and sighed. "And Otis? What does he think, exactly?"

Vikas dropped his gaze to the floor for a moment before meeting Vlad's eyes. "Perhaps that is a question best asked of your uncle."

Vlad handed the handkerchief back and stood. He'd half-expected Vikas to flinch when their fingers touched. "Tell me what you believe."

Vikas eyed him for a moment, and then said, "I believe that you are unique . . . and in the vampire world, that is a dangerous thing. But more than anything, I believe you are capable of more than your uncle credits you with. I would like to see you defend yourself against your enemies. That is, if you are able to."

"I don't have any enemies. I mean, there are these kids at school, but I'm dealing with it." Vlad thought about the slayer, Eddie, Bill, and Tom. He wasn't exactly Mr. Popularity lately, but he still wouldn't call them enemies. Well, except maybe Bill and Tom.

Vikas shook his head, his eyes once again grimly serious. "There are those who believe that the Pravus is a walking god among vampirekind—that the only way to prove his existence is to try to take his life and see if he survives unscathed. If he dies, they were wrong and perhaps the Pravus has not yet come—if indeed he ever will. But if he lives . . ."

This was the last thing he needed. "You mean some psycho may try to kill me just to see if I'm this Pravus thing some old prophecy talked about years ago?"

Vikas moved toward a separate door, clearly ready to retire for the evening. "Be careful, Vladimir. And listen to your uncle. He means well."

The door closed behind Vikas, and Vlad returned to his chair and turned back to the fire.

The Pravus. So that's what the *Encyclopedia Vampyrica* had been hiding from him in those paragraphs he couldn't seem to translate. A story about a vampire who would be born and was destined to reign over all of vampirekind, whether they liked it or not. His stomach twisted and turned. What if someone really did try to kill him just to see if he'd die? It was bad enough knowing some psycho slayer was hunting him, and that Eddie Poe was determined to weasel his opinion into the light of day, but now this. Vlad took a deep breath and let it out slowly, fighting to remain calm.

After a short time, and many more calming breaths, his eyes fluttered closed.

Otis woke him with a gentle shake. Vlad rubbed his eyes, sure that he could sleep for several more hours.

Otis smiled. His skin looked pink and healthy. "Go to bed, Vlad. That chair can't be comfortable."

Vlad nodded. He started to ask Otis if he thought Vlad was the vampire the prophecies spoke of but then closed his mouth again and shuffled off to his room.

If Otis did think he was the Pravus, Vlad didn't want to know.

14

TRAINING INTERRUPTED

FOCUS, MAHLYENKI DYAVOL." Vikas's voice brimmed with excitement, echoing only slightly through the darkness of the training room. They had been inside for over an hour, and neither seemed anxious to leave after so much success.

Vlad breathed in deeply and pictured rivers of deliciously sweet blood pouring over a hard edge, splashing into a pool of crimson below. His stomach tensed, and suddenly he could feel the power within him—just as Vikas had instructed him all week. It was there at his center, a hot, tingly ball of electricity resonating from his core. Delicious. Vlad surrendered himself to it, felt it coursing through his veins. Then he focused on Henry and pushed.

Henry smiled. It wasn't every day he got to spend a day hanging out on the slopes with his cousin and a gaggle of pretty girls. Not to mention a set of flirtatious, doe-eyed twins. Henry kept his cool and threw Joss a glance, raising his voice so the twins would hear. "Let's hit that black diamond."

As expected, Joss's jaw dropped. He had no idea how important it was to impress girls with your skills . . . even if you had only ever been on a black diamond trail twice in your life.

The twins grinned at Henry, and he turned with a casual step toward the slope, flashing his best smile briefly over his shoulder. If he played his cards right, there would be a fireplace and a set of matching snow bunnies in his near future. Smooth, Henry. Keep it smooth.

Vlad steadied his thoughts, smirked, and gently nudged.

Henry lost his footing and did a face plant in the snow.

Vlad would have remained in his mind to enjoy the laughter of Joss and the girls, but it was too hard to focus when he was laughing so hard himself. He pulled quickly out of Henry's mind, and Vikas's laughter joined his. "As I said, Vladimir, it is both productive and entertaining to read and control minds. Are you enjoying yourself?"

Vlad beamed into the darkness. "Absolutely. What's next?"

Vikas was quiet for a moment, and when he spoke, it was with hesitation. "Perhaps we could move on to something a bit more productive. Say . . . vengeance?"

Vlad swallowed, dropping his voice to nearly a whisper. "What do you mean exactly?"

"Only that I am sure there are certain wrongdoers in your life that have been long awaiting some payback for their actions against you. Am I wrong?"

Vlad didn't have to think hard. "No. But . . . what do you mean by revenge?"

Vikas's tone softened, but that didn't hide his eagerness. "Nothing more than a harmless prank. Of course, if you'd rather not pay them back for all that they've done to you . . ."

Vlad thought about Bill and Tom and every locker he'd ever been slammed into. He licked his lips slowly and said, "What do you have in mind?"

A knock at the door barely echoed into the room. Vlad relaxed his shoulders in disappointment. Their session was over—and before he could give Bill and Tom a taste of their own medicine.

Otis opened the door wide, spilling light into the room. "If I might steal my nephew away for a moment, Vikas."

Vikas nodded. "Certainly."

After a nod to Vikas, Vlad followed Otis out into the chilly air. The snow was blinding. He squinted and looked over at his uncle as they trekked up a nearby hill. "Is something wrong?"

Otis gave him a sideways glance. He pushed forward until they'd crested the hill. In front of them was a small clearing, untouched by footprints. Otis sighed. "What would make you think something was wrong?"

Vlad cleared his throat. He had the sneaking suspicion he was in trouble, but he wasn't sure why. "Well, you've never interrupted my training room sessions before."

Otis turned to face him, his lips pursed tightly. "It's just that I don't approve of today's lessons. Or rather, where today's lessons were turning to. Concepts like vengeance and humans used for amusement may suit some vampires, Vlad, but they hardly suit you."

Vlad paused, then lowered his voice suspiciously. "Those walls are thick enough to block out all sound, Otis. How did you know what we were talking about?"

Otis's steps slowed as they entered the clearing on the tree-topped hill. He dropped his gaze to the virgin snow on the ground. Vlad swore he could detect a hint of shame in his uncle's posture.

"You read my mind? I thought we had a deal!" Vlad's chest rose and fell as both his breathing and his heart rate picked up in irritation. "You stay out of my head, I stay out of yours, remember?"

Otis's eyes snapped back to Vlad's. His jaw tightened, as did his tone. "I remember all too well. Perhaps you'll do well to recall how unsettling it is to have someone wandering around in your head the next time you make Henry fall. Or worse. What were your plans for Bill and Tom exactly?"

Vlad dropped his eyes, but only for a second. "I wasn't going to hurt them or anything."

"If you give in to this urge, this yearning for vengeance, you'll find it only too easy to move from harmless prank to . . ." Otis broke off then. His eyes wore the look of some-one who has said too much.

Vlad tensed. With a stark eyebrow raised, he put a chill in his tone. "To enslaving the human race?"

Otis's eyes widened briefly with surprise, then darkened in defeat. His voice had dropped to a near whisper. "There are many steps between, but they are linked, Vlad. And closer than you realize, I assure you."

Vlad stood quiet for some time. His uncle had all but said he believed Vlad to be the Pravus. How could he think that? How could he believe that his only nephew was a monster? Vlad's chest ached, but he managed to keep the hurt out of his tone. "Otis, you're blowing this way out of proportion. Besides, you can't just come into my thoughts and not allow me into yours. Especially after our agreement."

"I was trying to protect you."

"From what? I thought you trusted Vikas to teach me."

"I do. It's just . . ." Otis shook his head, his anger visibly melting away. "Vikas is a traditional teacher. For the most part, his curriculum is brilliant. But some of his ideals are not necessarily the ideals I wish to instill in you."

Vlad chewed his bottom lip thoughtfully before speaking. "Shouldn't that be up to me?"

Otis met Vlad's eyes, wide and full of awe. "Such wisdom from someone so young." He shook his head and released a sigh, warming the chilled air between them. "I will interfere no more."

Vlad drew his collar up so that it touched his cheeks, and shivered, shuffling his feet in the crisp white powder. One thing was for sure: Otis could have picked a warmer place to lecture him. "Is that why you brought me out here?"

"Partially. I also wanted to give you a gift." Otis's eyes were careful. "Would you like to see your father again?"

Suddenly, Vlad wasn't cold anymore.

He looked at Otis, who merely nodded, as if to say that yes, it was possible. But it wasn't. Unless vampires could also travel through time. And if that were the case, Vlad was going to go back to the day he'd lost his parents and get them out of the house before the fire, save them, so that they would never have to be apart again. But . . . it wasn't possible. It couldn't be, or Otis would have told him already. "What are you—"

"It's simple. Tomas and I used to do this whenever we were apart, to catch one another up on moments we deemed important or memorable. It requires that you open your mind to me. . . ." A flash of guilt crossed Otis's eyes. "But trust that I will go no further than to share my memories with you. Your thoughts are safe. I swear that I will not tread there unwanted again."

"You mean I can see your memories of my dad?" At Otis's nod, Vlad's bottom lip trembled, but he bit it back into submission. "I would like that very much."

"Breathe deep, and open your mind." Otis locked eyes with him, his gaze fevered and intense. Vlad drew a long, slow, deep breath and tried not to think about anything in particular—just as Vikas had taught him.

At first, there was nothing. Just the uncluttered quiet of his mind.

And then . . .

A flash. A face. Familiar, warm, smiling. Then, just as quickly as it had come, it was gone again. Like a single frame of some old 8 mm film.

"Open, Vlad. Try not to focus."

Vlad steadied his breathing and waited.

The film reel in his mind flickered again, this time adding movement to his father's smiling face. The film jumped, and the image came into focus, surprising Vlad with the background noise of a busy marketplace. Tomas smiled at him—no, not at him . . . at Otis. He was seeing this through Otis's eyes—and laughed. "Come now, Otis. It's not like the Black Death is the end of the world. Lighten up."

Then, just as quickly as it had begun, the film ended, flipping forward through random pictures until it showed Tomas's laughing face once again. "It isn't every day we get a vegetarian meal, Otis."

Across the street sat a group of long-haired hippies. One strummed a guitar while the others sang some song about peace and love. Otis chuckled. Tomas licked his lips, his fangs slightly exposed. "They look a bit stringy, but I'm sure we could squeeze a drop or two out of them. What do you think?"

Tomas looked back at Otis then, and Vlad saw his twinkling eyes, the familiar way the corner of his mouth rose in a smirk . . . familiar, because Vlad's did that, too.

Vlad tried to speak but couldn't. It was just a memory, just a fixed picture inside Otis's head. He kept his mind open and watched the film jump through blurry images until it settled on another memory.

Tomas was at a library. A wall of books surrounded him as he pored through every page. Vlad watched him, the way he seemed unaware of anything but the words on the page—so like Vlad whenever he immersed himself in a really good book. It was startling how similar his dad's mannerisms were to his. Vlad knew he and his dad were alike, but he'd forgotten just how much.

Otis's voice broke in. "Reading, again? What this time?"

Tomas looked up, his intense focus broken by a surprised smile. "Just some old stories. To pass the time, you know. What about you? I thought you were on a plane to Siberia."

Otis's words were cut off by the film as it flipped once again through time.

Rain was pouring down in sheets, painting Tomas's hair to his skin. He looked over his shoulder at Otis, his eyes sincere. "We're brothers, Otis. We'll always be brothers."

The film reel slowed, and Vlad could feel Otis pulling out of his mind. But he wasn't ready yet. Not to let go of the few precious moments he'd witnessed. He needed more, just a few more. . . .

The film reel jumped in reverse. Once again, Tomas was standing in the rain. This time, his forehead was creased in anger. "I'm not asking you to lie, nor to put aside your prejudices, Otis. I merely wanted to say good-bye before I left."

"A human, Tomas. I understand the need to be loved, but to abandon all of Elysia for a human? That's madness." Otis shook his head. "Where will you go?"

"I dare not say."

"You don't trust me?"

Tomas paused and held Otis's gaze before turning away. "I dare not say."

"Fine. Go if you must. But don't ask me for help when this all comes crashing down around you." Otis's voice shook. "I feel like I don't even know you anymore."

Tomas looked over his shoulder at Otis, his eyes sincere. "We're brothers, Otis. We'll always be brothers."

Vlad furrowed his brow. The movie in his mind came to an end, and when he opened his eyes, Otis's forehead matched his. "Otis, I—"

"It's okay. You didn't know any better . . . and I didn't think you'd be able to pull the memory from me. It was the last day I saw your father. We fought. I was less than supportive of his romance with your mother, and I'm ashamed to admit, I was even less supportive when it came to Mellina's pregnancy." Shame washed over Otis's features, and when he met Vlad's eyes, Vlad had to bite his tongue to keep the tears at bay. "Forgive an old fool, Vlad. I had no idea at the time how much I would regret that my last moment with Tomas was an argument. Nor did I have any clue that I would come to care so deeply for his son."

Vlad dropped his gaze to the snow between his feet. In the past year, Otis had been something to him that only Tomas had been before—a father figure. A round tear betrayed him and rolled down his cheek, dripping from his chin to the snow below. "Thank you, Otis. For everything."

Otis seemed to swallow his own tears and looked down the hill at the small village. "You should get back to your lessons."

Vlad cleared his throat against his fist. "If you don't mind . . . I'd rather you showed me what ideals you want me to have."

Otis glanced back at him, his eyebrows raised. "You mean, teach you? Vlad, I'm not sure I'd be much of a teacher."

Vlad smirked, recalling the costumes and assignments of his eighth grade year. "You didn't do so bad last year."

"What do you want to learn?"

Vlad shrugged. The truth was he wanted to learn anything Otis was willing to teach him. More than that, he wanted to draw out this moment alone together. Learning from Vikas had been great, but Vlad missed his uncle . . . plus, he had the sneaking suspicion that once the trip was over, Otis would be gone again, traveling the world in search of assistance for their predicament. "How did you do that memory thing?"

"It's just an extension of sharing thoughts." His tone suggested it was no big deal. When he looked at Vlad, though, he seemed surprised. "Have you and Vikas not yet conversed telepathically?"

Vlad shook his head. Apparently, he wasn't learning as much as he thought from Vikas.

"Your father and I used to communicate by thought quite often. So often, in fact, that when he fled Elysia, I suffered migraines from the constant quiet in my mind." Otis smiled briefly, but his eyes betrayed a darkness that lurked within. "To speak telepathically is one of the most trusting actions a vampire can partake in, as you're allowing another to push into your mind at will. It's a delicate balance of give-and-take. I will keep my mind open to you, and you to me. If we focus on the meaning of our words rather than on the words themselves, they will translate into conversations in our minds that only we can hear. Over time, if you like, we should be able to communicate at great distance. Do you want to give it a try?"

"Definitely."

"Open your mind to me."

Vlad relaxed, closed his eyes—it was easier with closed eyes, he thought—and let go of any thoughts, any questions that were tangling up his mind, anxious to hear Otis's voice in his head, the way his father had on many occasions.

Otis's words came out in a hushed breath. "Good. Now, focus on the meaning of your words and push them into my mind gently."

"Like this?" His eyes flew open at his own words. They sounded different. Not muddled, really, but low, as if confined in a small space.

Otis's chuckle reverberated through Vlad's skull, a pleasant buzzing in his brain. *"Absolutely. It comes in handy when humans are around and we want to discuss things of vampiric nature. Pretty neat, eh?"*

Vlad's lips broke into a grin. *"This is way cooler than hovering. I can't wait to show Henry. Ought to make algebra class more interesting."*

Otis shook his head and spoke aloud. "Henry is human. He doesn't have the brainpower to receive such clear communication. You can read his thoughts easily, and even plant thoughts in his mind that lead him to wonder about certain things, driving his curiosity to the brink, where he is driven to follow where your planted thoughts lead, but you can never clearly communicate by thought with a human. Even a drudge like Henry."

Vlad's shoulders sank some. "That sucks."

"You're so like Tomas. Impatient with what skills you've been given and constantly longing for more." Otis chuckled, then patted Vlad on the back before turning and making his way down the hill. "Not necessarily a bad way to be."

Vlad hurried to keep up. "Is there anything else I'm missing out on? I mean, besides learning about telepathy and memory sharing."

Otis was quiet for several steps before sighing and shoving his hands into his coat pockets. "The truth is that I don't know what lies ahead for you, Vlad. As I told you before, you're one of a kind. No one but you has ever been born a vampire. We were all made, bitten by our creators, and given the essence of Elysia. The future for each of us is fairly certain. The future for you is not yet written. I could give you a list of skills that you may develop, but it would be senseless to speculate."

Vlad wanted to say that it wasn't senseless, that he had no idea what was coming for him, and he was pretty sure that a vampire going through puberty was a lot scarier than a human going through it. But Otis was already many steps in front of him, and he had the feeling his reasons would come out sounding like a whine, and that wasn't at all how he wanted to portray himself.

When he caught up to Otis outside the training room, he shoved his hands in his pockets, mimicking his uncle. "When we go back to Bathory, will you stay with me and Nelly?"

Otis sighed, and Vlad had his answer. His heart sank into his stomach and curled into a shriveled little ball. "I can't. Not yet. First I must convince Elysia that I am not a criminal, that my actions were necessary, and that will take time. If I could get three of the councils on my side, I might be able to make my case. But until I convince them of my good intentions, I'm afraid moving to Bathory is out of the question. I cannot risk your and Nelly's lives."

"But I have the Lucis. I could protect you." Vlad reached into his jeans pocket to withdraw the weapon, but Otis grabbed him by the wrist and shook his head carefully.

"Not here, Vlad. Keep it hidden."

Vlad nodded slowly, and Otis relaxed his grip.

"The Lucis may be what protects you from the so-called justice of Elysia, Vlad. But I am well known . . . as are the details of my supposed crimes. It would not be enough to keep them from tearing that town apart to find me. Bathory is just too close to Stokerton to risk moving to—even with the aid of a Tego charm, I'm not nearly as brave as your father was to try hiding there."

Vlad shoved the Lucis deeper into his pocket. "Tego charm?"

"A charm used to block telepathy. You'll learn more about this later on, as well as how to utilize your mark."

Otis's serious pursed lips relaxed into a smile then. "The most wonderful things await you. A lifetime of learning, experiences unlike any other, and worlds that you have not yet dared to dream. Just wait until you feed from the source. . . ."

"I'll never do that." Vlad met Otis's eyes. "I won't."

Otis shrugged, as if to say "maybe you will, maybe you won't," and opened the door to the training room. His uncle's passivity irritated Vlad, though he wasn't sure why, exactly.

He stepped inside and had time enough to notice Vikas before the door closed behind him, sealing them in the darkness once again.

15
WHERE THE HEART IS

V LAD SAT UP IN bed and stretched. He was in no hurry to place his feet on the chilly floor, but it was his last day in Siberia, in Elysia, and if he stayed in bed, he'd never go home. He and Vikas had spent several long days inside the darkened, silent room, and Vlad had opened up to the possibilities that mind control, when used with honorable purpose, could be a handy skill to possess. In the room, he was great at it. Vlad once made Tristian take a break from his duties and, much to Vikas's bemusement, he made one of the vampires burst into song. But it was hard work, not to mention exhausting. Plus, it was almost impossible for him to control anyone's mind once outside of the training room.

When he told Vikas about having made Henry pick his nose once, Vikas explained that a drudge is the easiest person for a vampire to control. After he stopped laughing, of course.

His telepathy was coming along fabulously as well. He and Otis engaged in long conversations at night near the hearth, where Otis recounted tales of Vlad's father. Vlad was learning so much about a man that he really hadn't known that well. And through those stories, he was learning more about Otis as well.

Cringing at the cold floor, Vlad stood and dressed quickly. You'd think that after a week in one of the coldest places on Earth, he'd adjust, but apparently not. He shivered once and reached for his hoodie.

He opened the door to the main room, and Tristian met him with a goblet of bloodwine. Vlad nodded his thanks and sighed into the cup. He was really tired of spiced blood. What he really wanted was a nice warm mug of O positive and a side of fresh chocolate chip cookies.

Otis stood by the front door, brushing snow from his coat. "We should leave soon, Vlad. A storm is blowing in, and Vikas said that if it gets to us before we make it down the mountain, we'll have a long winter season in Siberia ahead of us."

Vlad yawned. "Can I finish my breakfast first?"

Otis nodded.

Vlad looked to the fireplace. The logs had grown cold. The room was empty, except for him, Otis, and Tristian.

After a silent moment, Otis cleared his throat. "Most of them have gone to bed. Vikas is out running with the wolves, he said he'd be back in time to see us off."

Vlad drained his goblet and sat on the nearby table. "He's running with the wolves?"

Otis waved his hand in the air, as if it were obvious what Vikas was up to. "One of the intricacies of animorphing is spending so much time with an animal that you understand their desires, their thought processes." Then he smirked and handed Vlad his coat. "Besides, he likes to chase foxes."

Vlad slipped his coat on, zipped it, and stomped into his boots. Animorphing. That was something the book hadn't mentioned. In fact, the book had only really covered history and laws, leaving out all the cool stuff, as if any vampire should be aware of those things automatically. Of course, Vlad mused, he wasn't just any vampire.

Just outside the door, Vikas greeted them breathlessly. His eyes sparkled sadly at Otis. "Too bad about that storm. It's been an eternity since I saw you last."

Otis pursed his lips. "I can't stay. But I do hope you'll at least reconsider my request. We are old friends, Vikas. If I can't count on you, who can I count on?"

Vikas held Otis's gaze, then nodded and patted him roughly on the shoulder. He turned to Vlad. "You are one of my finest students. Keep practicing, and stay with your studies. Be safe, Mahlyenki Dyavol. We will meet again someday, I am sure of it."

Otis stepped onto the sled.

Vlad watched Vikas walk away into the blowing snow. "I've decided I like that nickname."

Otis cleared his throat and pulled goggles down over his eyes, but it was too late—Vlad had already spotted his tears. "It suits you. Vikas's pet name for Tomas was Dyavol . . . Devil. So, I suppose, it's his way of saying that you're a smaller version of your father."

Vlad took his seat on the sled, but he didn't pull the blanket up to his nose. The wind was blowing all around. The temperature had dropped to a chill rivaling last night's. But Vlad was warm with the memory of his father and the fact that a Russian stranger had seen Tomas within him.

The sled raced down the mountain, past trees, wildlife, and snow. By the time they'd turned the dogs over to Dmitri, took a cab to the airport, and boarded the plane, Vlad was exhausted, and Otis was tense, the relaxation of being in Elysia washing away from him with every passing moment.

Vlad flashed him a smile. "Thanks for taking me to meet Vikas. He was pretty cool."

"He cares a great deal for you already, Vlad. I'm glad you enjoyed his company."

Vlad ran the tip of his tongue slowly over his chapped lips and said, "He told me about the Pravus."

Otis's entire body went rigid with tension. "Did he?"

Despite Otis's tone, it wasn't a question.

Vlad unbuckled and turned to face his uncle. "Yeah. It's crazy. I mean, me? Some evil conqueror? I don't think so. But I was wondering . . . well . . ." Vlad fidgeted. He wanted to know what Otis thought, but at the same time, he didn't.

Otis met his eyes. "You're wondering if I think you're the Pravus."

Vlad nodded and held Otis's gaze.

Otis shook his head, his expression gravely serious. "No, I do not believe you are the Pravus, Vladimir. You have too much of your father in you. And Tomas was a good man."

Vlad searched his uncle's eyes and found nothing but truth within them.

"The question is . . . do you think you're the Pravus?"

Otis's voice was calm and questioning inside Vlad's mind. Vlad took a moment to mull over his opinion and then spoke to Otis with his thoughts. *"No. I don't. But if I was, would it matter?"*

A pretty flight attendant leaned over Vlad and handed Otis a cup of coffee. Otis smiled at her and took a polite sip. *"Of course not. Besides, it's just a silly superstition."*

Vlad tried to meet Otis's eyes, but Otis focused on his coffee, and the conversation was over.

After hours of planes, baggage, crowds, rushing, and Otis losing his keys, they were finally in Otis's hunk-of-junk car and barreling toward Bathory. At last, Otis turned the wheel and pulled into Nelly's driveway. He met Vlad's eyes with a smile. "Happy to be home?"

"Kind of. Tired. Hungry, more than anything."

Otis opened his car door and stepped out. Vlad followed. He was about to ask Otis if he planned on sticking around for a few days, when he noticed a flash of pink out of the corner of his eye.

Meredith was walking up the driveway with his jacket draped over her arm. She smiled brightly and said, "Hi, Vlad. Oh, hello, Mr. Otis!"

Otis removed the heavier suitcase from the trunk and smiled. "Hello, Meredith. How are you doing?"

Meredith shrugged. "Can't complain. Miss having you as a teacher, though."

Vlad's cheek grew very warm at the memory of Meredith's kiss. When he thought about how he'd blurted out that he liked her, and how warm her lips had been in the freezing cold, he couldn't speak. His heart had returned to his throat, intent on choking him into silence.

"I assure you, there are better teachers than I at Bathory High." To Vlad, Otis looked like a lifeguard to a drowning man as Otis took Vlad's coat from Meredith's outstretched hand. "Thank you so much for returning Vladimir's jacket. I imagine he appreciates it greatly."

Vlad managed a nod. His entire face felt like it had been engulfed in flames.

Meredith and Otis exchanged pleasantries before Meredith turned and walked away. After she did, Otis handed Vlad the jacket with a smirk. "Charm, Vladimir, requires a voice."

Nelly stepped out onto the porch, wrapped snugly in her coat. "I was wondering when you boys would get here. Staying for dinner, Otis?"

Otis handed Vlad one of the bags and smiled warmly up at Nelly. All traces of tension vanished. "I wouldn't dream of missing it, Nelly."

With a blush, Nelly went back inside.

Vlad shook his head and rolled his eyes, but he couldn't help but smile. "You like her, don't you, Otis?"

Otis looked jarred for a moment. He kept his attention on the front door, as if weighing how much he should reveal to Vlad. It was a pitiful sight, as Vlad already knew the answer. Otis sighed and ran a hand through his hair in defeat. "Yes."

Vlad lugged a bag toward the porch, still smiling. He cast a hopeful glance over his shoulder at Otis. "So does that mean you'll be around more?"

Otis sat the bag he was carrying on the porch and offered Vlad a somber look. "No, it does not."

Vlad's smile slipped in disappointment.

"A romance with Nelly is forbidden for me. You know that. It's unfortunate"—he glanced up at the house and back to Vlad—"but unavoidable. Besides, Elysia has enough reasons to place a price on my head."

"Is that why you stay away?" Vlad dropped his bag on the porch and turned to Otis, an accusing look in his eyes.

"I only stay away in order to seek assistance for my—our—predicament, Vlad. I would do anything to protect you from harm."

Vlad shrugged. "Couldn't you protect me better if you were closer?"

The crease in Otis's forehead deepened. He looked angry, but Vlad wasn't sure why. "Suffice it to say that I have bled for your well-being, Vladimir. And I will gladly do so again."

Vlad nodded, his curiosity satisfied for the moment. "Will we ever be able to be together, like a family?"

"Perhaps, one day." Otis sighed. "Once the council elects a new president, things could change. But as the death of a president is so unlikely, it is also something that the council isn't well prepared for. It may be a year. It may be ten. It may be a hundred years. With any luck, the new president will be sympathetic to our plight."

"And until then?"

"I run from them. And keep my distance from you." Otis offered a troubled frown. "I'm sorry, Vladimir. It's just the way things are. For now."

Vlad sighed. "So, I'm on my own."

"Not entirely. We'll still have letters and, if you're able to reach the distance, we can continue to communicate with our thoughts."

Otis grabbed the larger suitcase and headed up the steps to the door. After a moment, Vlad followed.

Nelly already had their plates filled with delicious, warm steaks, dripping with blood. Vlad took a swig of B negative from his glass and listened as Otis relayed details of their trip. Well, not details. Not really. Otis carefully omitted that they'd stayed with other vampires and that Vlad had learned that there are vampires who believe he was some demon-like beast come to reign over vampirekind. Vlad was thankful for that at least.

But he did speak lovingly of the countryside and of how much he'd enjoyed the trip. Vlad wondered if Otis was trying to reassure him that he cared, but there was no need. He knew his uncle cared for him. How can you go through hours on a dogsled through Siberia just to seek out protection and tutoring for somebody and *not* care for them?

After dinner and after whispered, too-close good-byes with Nelly, Otis slipped his top hat onto his head and walked her out to the car. Minutes later, Nelly drove in the direction of the hospital for yet another double shift, and Vlad moved down the steps toward Otis. "When will I see you again?"

"In all honesty, I do not know. But I hope it's soon." Otis hugged him and slid into the driver's seat. He looked up at

Vlad with a wrinkled brow. "If you have any troubles, call for me with your mind. If I don't respond, write me. And should you encounter the slayer, my best advice is to block the stake—they favor those—and run as fast as you can."

Vlad sighed. "That's your best advice?"

Otis chuckled. "Sadly, yes. The Lucis has no effect on humans. You'll do fine. Just lay low. He may leave without discovering you. Most slayers are poorly paid and easily distracted. Bumbling fools, the lot of them." He pulled the car door shut and, after two attempts to start it, backed onto the road and drove off down the street.

Vlad stayed where he was and watched the taillights of Otis's car shrink in the distance. He missed his uncle already.

It was still late afternoon, and the sun had not yet set. Across the street, Mr. Templeton was shoveling snow from the sidewalk and tossing it onto his snow-blanketed yard. Several elementary school kids were building a snow fort two houses down and filling the air with blissful laughter. Mr. Jenkins, the mailman, walked by and offered Vlad a nod as he shoved a small pile of letters into the mailbox. Vlad watched them all with a distant curiosity.

As he turned his head back to the direction Otis had driven, he noticed a man standing across the street, staring directly at him. At first Vlad merely raised his eyebrows. He wasn't a teacher, Vlad was almost certain. And he knew pretty much everyone in Bathory, if only by face. He watched the man watching him and tilted his head to the side, wondering where he'd seen this man before.

The man stepped forward, and halfway across the street, he broke into a run.

And then it hit Vlad. It was the man who'd been standing across the street that night after Vlad had left the belfry. The one Vlad felt certain was the slayer.

Everything but the man and Vlad slowed to a crawl. He blinked as the slayer approached, and Vlad threw his arms up to block the stake he was sure the slayer had behind his back. He backed away as fast as he could.

The laughter of the kids down the street sounded like a slow, muffled recording, and Mr. Templeton was shoveling at a tenth of the speed he'd been. There was no time to run. The slayer was moving faster than sound.

The man opened his mouth wide, exposing glistening white fangs.

Vlad dropped his arms in confusion. Fangs?

A searing pain lit up Vlad's neck as the vampire bit into his artery. Vlad felt a sudden ache tear through him as the blood was sucked from his veins. He gasped, more surprised than scared, and forgot to fight back.

Vlad watched his neighbors moving in that weird slow motion that had overtaken them. Why couldn't they see the vampire attacking him? The answer was simple. Some vampires were apparently gifted with the ability to move so fast that humans couldn't see.

Huh. That wasn't in the book. He'd have to remember that trick the next time Bill and Tom came around.

If there was a next time.

The vampire pulled away and withdrew a glass tube from his jacket's inside pocket. He spit a mouthful of Vlad's blood into it and capped it with a cork.

Vlad clutched his neck, suddenly very woozy and still lacking the urge to fight. He wondered if that was an effect of being drunk from so deeply. He pushed weakly with his thoughts to call for Otis, but he could barely focus on his uncle's name. He forced his attention back on his attacker. "Who are you?"

The vampire smirked. "I am Jasik."

Vlad's head swam. He was dying. Holy crap, he was dying . . . and it was a vampire who was killing him.

He stumbled, dizzy from blood loss, but tried hard not to fall over into the freshly fallen snow. "Are you . . . are you going to kill me, Jasik?"

Jasik's metallic laughter filled Vlad's ears. "No, little one. I am no killer—there are laws, remember? I am but a thief." He held up the vial for Vlad to see and then slipped it into his jacket pocket.

Blood squeezed out from between Vlad's fingers. His wound was taking its time to heal. What was that chemical mosquitoes used to keep blood flowing from their victims? He'd just read about it in science class.

Anticoagulant. Mr. Gaunt would be proud.

"Jasik." Vlad wavered and finally collapsed on the ground. He thought he asked his attacker "do you feel bad?" before he passed out, but he couldn't be certain.

What he did know was that he heard Jasik's laughter again and watched his footprints in the snow as he walked away.

16

THE HEALING POWER OF BLOOD

VLAD'S HEAD FELT LIKE it was being crushed by a large rock. He tried to lift it, but it was pinned to the pillow. Pillow?

He cracked open one eye and looked up at a very concerned-looking Henry. He tried to open his other eye but couldn't, so he gave up and closed them. Henry shook him gently. "Hey, are you okay?"

He licked his lips and forced open his eye again. This time the other eye opened, too. "Henry?"

Henry nodded, a dark cloud of concern hanging over him. "I had this weird feeling like you were in trouble, so I came over and found you lying facedown in your driveway, surrounded by a bunch of your neighbors. Mr. Templeton said he was gonna call 911, but I stopped him."

"How'd you manage that? He's got to be the most stubborn old man on the planet."

"I told him that you'd been sick with the flu and that I was supposed to be looking in on you while Nelly was at work. I said I'd call her as soon as I got you inside."

Vlad bit his bottom lip and gave Henry a pensive glance. "Did you call her?"

Henry shook his head. "Nah. I wanted to talk to you first. What happened?"

Vlad tried once more to lift his head but failed. He took a deep breath. His skin felt like it was on fire. What had happened? His memory was fuzzy at first, but then he remembered fangs and a flash of pain. Jasik had been his attacker's name. Vlad reached up to his neck. The puncture wounds had already healed, leaving only smooth skin behind. In a disbelieving voice, Vlad said, "A vampire bit me."

Henry rolled his eyes. "Funny."

"I'm serious."

Henry looked him over for a moment, and then nodded. "Any idea who it was?"

"He said his name was Jasik. I've never seen him before." Vlad thought for a moment and then met Henry's eyes. "What did it feel like when I drank from you?"

Henry thought for a moment, and then said, "Like a paper cut, to be honest. Your fangs were really sharp, so the bite made me wince, but after that it was okay. It was a little dizzying once you started drinking, but not painful or anything. Why?"

Vlad rubbed his neck where Jasik had bitten him. "When Otis gave me my mark last year, it barely hurt. I felt a little dizzy, but that was it. I wonder why when Jasik bit me it hurt so much and left me feeling so weak."

"Well, you just tasted my blood, and Otis was just taking some of yours. Maybe this Jasik guy took more." Henry's voice shook some. "Maybe he was trying to kill you."

"No. He said he was a thief, not a killer." Vlad lifted his head and tried to sit up, but he was overcome by the most nauseating dizziness, so he lay back down.

"Can you sit up?" Apparently, Henry had amazing powers of intuition.

"No." Vlad gestured to the door with his eyes. "I need blood."

With an assenting nod, Henry moved out Vlad's bedroom door. Vlad heard him cross the library and move down the stairs. The house was quiet for a moment, and then Henry jogged his way back up the stairs and into Vlad's room. He laid an armful of blood bags on the bed. "There were four in the freezer. I brought them all."

Vlad brought one bag up to his mouth and bit into it. It was only then that he realized his fangs had elongated.

He sucked the bag dry and reached for another, continuing until they were all empty. But something was missing. He should feel better but didn't. Vlad squeezed his eyes shut and opened them again. "I feel weird."

"Well, you are weird."

"My heart is racing, and I can't pick up my head without getting dizzy." Vlad licked his lips, relieved that it had been Henry who'd found him passed out in the driveway. He met Henry's eyes. "I'm pretty sure I need more blood. Man, how much did he drink, anyway?"

Henry slipped his cell phone out of his pocket. "I'm calling Nelly."

"No!" Vlad made a feeble grab for the phone, as if that could stop Henry from calling. He cast Henry a worried glance. "You can't call her. She'll worry."

Henry sighed and sat the phone on the bed. "Vlad, another vampire just tried to have you for dinner. We have to tell someone, and I'm pretty sure the Red Cross doesn't handle these types of situations."

Vlad licked the holes in the last blood bag clean and lied, "I'll be fine."

He didn't know if he'd be fine or not. The whole experience made him feel extra guilty for having ever bitten Henry.

Still, he couldn't deny how hungry he was.

Henry was quiet for a moment, then rolled up his sleeve and held his arm out to Vlad with determination in his eyes. "Take some from me."

Vlad shook his head. "No."

A large blue vein drew a delicious line down Henry's arm. Vlad looked away.

Henry met his eyes. "Hey, what good is being your drudge if I don't have your back when you need it?"

Vlad tried hard to ignore the scent of Henry's blood. He thought of Tristian and the way Vikas barely looked at him. "I don't think of you that way, you know . . . like my slave. You're my best friend."

Henry smiled. "I know. Now shut up and drink my blood before I change my mind. Geez—there's nothing worse than a sappy overlord."

Vlad pursed his lips. "No, Henry."

"Vlad, I've wanted to tell you something since the third grade." Henry smirked and moved his arm closer. "Bite me."

Vlad looked at Henry's vein again and shivered. It looked warm, inviting, and delectable. He flipped open Henry's cell phone and punched in the number to the hospital. "Hey, Aunt Nelly. Could you come home real quick and bring me some blood? We're out."

Henry slowly unrolled his sleeve and whispered, "What are you going to tell her about the other vampire?"

Vlad covered the mouthpiece. "Nothing. And neither are you."

Relief left Henry's eyes, replaced by bemusement. "Yes, master."

17
TRAPPED

VLAD'S STOMACH WAS RUMBLING again, and it was taking every ounce of focus he had to keep his fangs in check. Clearly, lunch hadn't been enough, and his bloodthirst was getting the better of him. Maybe he needed to start sneaking extra snacks in during the day . . . or maybe get a note from Nelly saying he had to stop at the house for his "medication" for about ten minutes every afternoon. Either way, something had to be done to curb his appetite . . . and it had to be done fairly quickly.

His eyebrows scrunched together in irritation as Stephanie Brawn, cheerleader extraordinaire and kisser of all boys with a pulse, sashayed over to his locker. "Hi, Vlad."

He didn't reply—he'd known Stephanie far too long to trust her motives—but instead, he ducked his head inside his locker and pretended to be busy looking for something. He didn't know what, but he was sure that he wouldn't find whatever it was until Stephanie had seen something shiny and followed it down the hall.

Unfortunately, there must have been a distinct lack of shiny objects in the hall that day, because Stephanie wasn't going anywhere. "Did you see the senior lockers? They're painting them black and red, can you imagine? But then, I suppose it says something for school pride to use our colors."

Vlad sighed and pulled his head out of his locker far enough to raise an eyebrow at her. "Are we supposed to be friends or something? Because I missed that memo."

Stephanie's eyes grew wide in that fake way they always did when she was trying to impress a new teacher. "I'm just trying to reach out."

Vlad rolled his eyes. "Well, don't, okay? My life is complex enough without you trying to befriend me with some lame freshman outreach program."

"Don't you mean dork outreach program?" She smirked and moved her eyes to something behind Vlad, but it was too late for him to turn.

In a moment, Tom had Vlad pinned against his locker while Bill whaled away on Vlad's back with his fists. Vlad cried out in surprise and wondered for a second if Joss would save him this time, but then Tom picked him up by his shoulders and carried him down the hall, stopping only to toss him through a small door and down several steps. With laughter and taunts of, "Have fun, ladies!" Bill and Tom shut the door as Vlad landed on the bottom step of the boiler room.

The moment Vlad stopped rolling, he groaned, clutched his side, and slowly got to his feet. His back throbbed where Bill had pounded it, but his side hurt more—likely from his tumble down the stairs. He'd made his way back up to the door when a small voice called from below. "Don't bother. They'll block it from the outside, just like they did before."

Vlad tried the door, but it wouldn't budge. Running the tip of his tongue over his canines, he turned and made his way down the stairs. Eddie Poe was sitting on the floor, with his back against the wall, adjusting the cracked lens of his camera. Vlad wondered if it had broken during Eddie's tumble down the stairs. "So how long have you been down here, Eddie?"

Eddie shrugged, not meeting Vlad's eyes. "Since this morning."

Vlad glanced up at the door. He really didn't want to spend his day trapped in a glorified, hot-as-Hades basement—least of all with a boy who was on the verge of learning his deepest, darkest secret. His stomach rumbled, as if reminding him about his appointment with a blood bag. "Have you tried banging on the door, getting someone's attention?"

At the sound of Vlad's voice, Eddie flinched. A shard of glass fell from his camera lens to the floor, eliciting a groan. "Tried that. It's pretty soundproof. You know, to keep out the noise of the boiler and stuff."

Vlad looked around the room. There was nothing in it that would prove even mildly helpful for their escape. The best they could hope for was that Mr. Brennan, the school janitor, would have to check some gauges or something and would unwittingly come to their rescue. With a sigh, Vlad sat on the bottom step and ran a frustrated hand through his hair, brushing it out of his eyes for a moment.

Eddie met Vlad's eyes once, and then dropped his attention to the floor. He didn't look happy to be sharing the space with a monster.

Vlad forced a smile. He wasn't exactly pleased with the arrangement himself, but if he played his cards right, maybe he could have Eddie convinced he was nothing but human by the time the door opened. "So, that was some article you wrote. I didn't know you were a writer."

Eddie was quiet for a long time. And just as Vlad was about to ask him if he'd been kicked off the school paper, Eddie stood up and stretched. When he was finished, he cast a nervous glance up at the door and then returned his gaze to the floor. When he spoke, it was so low that Vlad had to strain in order to discern words from the whisper of Eddie's breath. "I always knew you were different. But I thought you were just an outcast, like me."

Vlad's lungs locked for a moment, refusing to allow air either in or out. There was no question in Eddie's slumped posture, or an ounce of doubt in his words. He knew Vlad's secret.

The air returned to Vlad's lungs in a gulp. He couldn't speak. What do you say to someone who's not just guessing but has witnessed your deepest secret in action? Vlad looked back over his shoulder at the door and sighed, wondering how long they'd already been down here. He imagined it was nearing the final bell, but without a watch, it was difficult to tell. His stomach rumbled loudly, demanding to be satisfied, and Vlad groaned. Great. Just what he needed. Trapped in a room with a human when he was thirsting for blood.

To Vlad's immense surprise, Eddie met his eyes. "I still don't know what you are exactly. But I read a lot of comic books, so I know I can figure it out."

He straightened his shoulders, a thread of confidence creeping into his words. "Your eyes flashing purple were the first solid clue that you weren't human, and then when I followed you to the school and you floated up to the belfry . . . well, I kind of freaked out at first. But I was smart. My mom says I'm not, but I am. I waited and took that picture of you coming down. I could have named you in the article, but right now I just want to find out what you are. I thought maybe you'd tell me after you saw the article."

Vlad shook his head. "There's nothing to tell, Eddie. I don't know who or what you saw, but I'm as human as anybody in this town." When he looked once more at Eddie, he made sure his words were crisp and forceful. "You should be more careful, dude. Stuff like that could get you kicked off the paper. Or worse."

Vlad held his gaze, making certain the threat was understood. He was tempted to try mind control, but he knew he didn't need to go that far with Eddie Poe. The guy always backed down when confronted. Always.

As suspected, Eddie's eyes widened in fear. Eddie took a step back, and when he bumped into the wall, he slid down to a sitting position on the floor, his arms clutching his knees to his chest. He watched Vlad for the next several minutes, as if frightened that Vlad might pounce on him and drink his blood.

Ready to oblige, Vlad's fangs slid easily out of his gums. It took several deep breaths, but after a moment, he regained control of his hunger. One thing was for sure though . . . if he didn't get out of here soon, Eddie was going to be his next meal.

With a deep breath, Vlad focused on Henry. He had no idea if he was capable of reaching his drudge from anywhere other than the training room in Siberia, but he had to try.

"Henry, I'm trapped in the boiler room with Eddie Poe. Hurry!"

Eddie continued to watch him. Vlad shifted uneasily but said nothing. After all, there was nothing to say. What was that saying about how it was better to be thought a fool, than to open your mouth and remove all doubt?

The door at the top of the stairs creaked open, startling them both. But then Vlad sighed in relief. He'd reached Henry after all. He made a mental note to write Otis and tell him. Apparently, Vikas was right about the ease of connecting with one's drudge.

Sunlight drifted in from the open door, illuminating the room much better than the fluorescent lights below. Meredith called down the steps. "Vlad? Are you down there?"

Vlad's eyes went wide, and he felt his hunger give way to the happy warmth of the knowledge that Meredith hadn't just opened the door by accident—she'd opened it because she'd been looking for him.

Vlad cleared his throat, only slightly disappointed that he hadn't managed to reach Henry. "Yeah."

Eddie slid his back against the wall as he stood. He approached the steps slowly, his eyes still locked distrustfully, fearfully, on Vlad. But then he paused and looked longingly up at the stairs.

Vlad stepped back, giving Eddie free passage. He kept his jaw tight and his gaze slightly chilled in warning.

Eddie glanced down at his shoes, and when he returned his eyes to Vlad's gaze, he seemed to be surer of himself than ever. He spoke in a loud whisper, so that Meredith wouldn't hear. "It's worth another detention, Vlad. It's worth a thousand detentions to find out what you are." He scrambled up the steps, then paused and threw Vlad a determined glance over his shoulder. "And worse."

He shrank by Meredith without meeting her eyes. Meredith smiled at him. "Hi, Eddie. You okay?"

But Eddie didn't answer.

Vlad moved up a few steps, shaking his anger with Eddie from his nerves. In his mind he was reliving the kiss Meredith had given him outside in the snow and the blowing cold. He wondered, briefly, if she might do it again if they lingered down here for a while. "Thanks for opening the door. We were kind of stuck."

A small flash of anger crossed Meredith's eyes, surprising him. "I heard Bill and Tom bragging about locking you guys down here. So I came to see if you were still here. What jerks!"

Vlad smiled. She was so cute when she was mad. The way her nose scrunched up.

Meredith looked at him. "What are you smiling about?"

Vlad glanced away. "Nothing. I'm just glad to see you."

She brightened, and Vlad widened his eyes. "I mean, the door. I'm glad you opened the door."

"Oh." A small smile played on her lips. "Well, you're welcome."

Though Vlad's cheeks were blushing fiercely, he managed a smile. "Yeah . . . my hero."

The air suddenly seemed very thin. Meredith was standing just one step above him and looking at him like he was the only boy in the entire world.

Vlad wanted very much to be brave enough to kiss her pretty lips.

He wanted to be. But he wasn't.

Instead, he smiled into her eyes and wished that the moment would last.

"Uh. Hey, Vlad . . . Meredith." Henry was standing at the open door, fighting a grin. "You guys better get out of here. Mrs. Bell is on her way down the hall, and she's giving out detention slips like crazy."

Meredith blushed and walked up the steps. After a second, Vlad followed suit, not really caring if he got detention.

All things considered, losing a few hours after school was well worth a stolen moment alone with the girl of his dreams.

18
THE FRIEND CODE

VLAD DESCENDED THE STEPS in front of Bathory High after a horrendous Monday. After a moment, Joss joined him, despite the chilly glances Vlad had been giving him since the Snow Ball. Yes, Meredith had kissed him and not Joss, but that didn't change the fact that Joss had gone out with her. They were supposed to be friends, and friends can tell when a guy likes a girl, even without the guy saying something. Even Henry had figured it out, and Vlad hadn't told him—Henry could just tell. So why couldn't Joss?

It was an exceptionally warm March day, so Vlad slipped off his jacket and draped it over his arm. March. He could hardly believe that he hadn't heard from his uncle Otis in three months, ever since the day they'd parted after their trip to Siberia. Vlad had written Otis immediately following Jasik's attack and had continued to do so once a week in increasingly worried tones, but he'd heard nothing back. At least the months since the attack had been blissfully free of Jasik, and there had been no sign of the slayer Otis had warned him about. But there was always the possibility that Otis had received misinformation. What if there was no slayer? What if it was just Jasik, the thief, in Bathory? Still, Vlad had kept close to his house and the school, never going anywhere alone, just to be safe. And he continued to worry about Otis.

They walked between houses, leaving Henry behind at the school for yet another student council meeting. Before they could move out from between the houses directly across the street from Nelly's, Joss hesitated and croaked, "I need to talk to you."

He looked pleadingly at Vlad, but there was no way Vlad was going to make it any easier on him. Dude. Friend code. Violated. Joss would have to deal.

Joss took a deep breath, steadied himself, and said, "I feel terrible about what I did to you. I knew you liked Meredith, but when she asked me to the dance, I couldn't believe it. She's just so pretty and funny and smart and—"

"Not helping the situation." Vlad pursed his lips, picturing the first time he'd seen Meredith. They were in the third grade, and Meredith was the new kid. She stood in front of the class, all scared and timid, twisting the pink ribbon in her hair tightly around her fingertip. She'd looked so frightened. All Vlad had wanted to do was to take her hand and protect her.

"I'm sorry, okay? I was way wrong. And now I feel like I've screwed up our friendship and I feel terrible, Vlad." Joss met Vlad's gaze with honest eyes. "Please. There's gotta be something I can do to make this up to you."

Vlad adjusted the strap of his backpack on his shoulder and tensed his jaw, still angry. "Next time you think I like someone, don't ignore that thought, okay? You really hurt my feelings, Joss. I thought we were friends."

"We are." Joss dropped his bag on the ground, his cheeks flushing some. "To be honest, other than Henry, you're my only friend . . . and he's family. If he doesn't hang out with me, his mom will ground him."

Vlad groaned as a sudden, unexpected flash of guilt shot through him. "That's not why he hangs out with you, Joss. Henry likes you. We both think you're pretty cool . . . when you're not dating girls we like." He sighed and dropped his backpack next to Joss's. Maybe he'd been too hard on Joss. Maybe he could consider this time served. After all, in the end, all Joss was guilty of was accepting an invitation to the dance. "Look, I haven't even told Henry how much I really like Meredith. And when you went to the dance with her . . . it just felt like you took our friendship and flushed it. That's hard to get over."

"I'll never do anything like that again. I swear, okay?" Joss sighed, a cloud of lost cause hanging over him. "Can we be friends again?"

Vlad ran a hand through his hair, brushing it away from his eyes, and mentally kicked himself. A large part of him wanted to hold this grudge forever, but he knew he couldn't. This was Joss. He was almost as important to Vlad as Henry. "We never stopped being friends. Just because I'm mad at you doesn't mean we're not friends."

Immense relief crossed Joss's eyes. Both boys were silent awhile until Joss cleared his throat. "So you really like her, huh?"

Vlad released a tense breath. He felt like he'd been holding it in since he heard about Meredith's Snow Ball plans. "Yeah. I do."

Joss eyed him for a moment, then said, "That took a lot of trust, spilling your guts like that."

"Well, I trust you." Vlad shrugged, suddenly feeling lighter, better after clearing the air.

"I trust you, too, Vlad." Joss grew quiet then, and when he spoke again, his voice shook slightly. "In fact, I've got a secret. A big one. One that I'd like to share with you. Is that okay?"

Vlad nodded. "Fine by me. Is it something bad?"

"No. Not really. I mean, I'm really proud of it. I just don't get to talk about it much. Plus, it's tied to a real problem I have, and I've been thinking maybe you could help me with that."

Vlad waited, but Joss didn't continue. "I can't help if you don't tell me."

"I will. It's just . . . hard, you know? I never tell anyone. And I need to talk to someone. And you . . . you know the town, the people. You have an open mind, judging by your book collection. I feel like I can trust you, like I finally have a friend that I'm not related to." He looked over his shoulder and then past Vlad, as if making certain they were alone. "I'm almost out of time. If I don't finish soon . . . I could be in serious trouble."

Vlad wrinkled his brow. Something in the pit of his stomach lurched forward, almost sending him off balance. It was his nerves. Something felt . . . wrong. "Dude, what's up? Is everything okay?"

By the look on Joss's face, everything most certainly was not okay. He licked his lips and flashed a nervous glance over his shoulder again. "I need your help."

Vlad wasn't entirely sure he wanted to hear whatever it was that Joss wanted to tell him, especially the more Joss rambled. His nerves moved and clenched, tying his stomach into tight, nervous knots.

Joss leaned in, keeping his voice low. "Listen, I'm seriously breaking protocol by telling you this. Hell, I broke protocol by coming here in the first place. Private gigs are prohibited. What was I thinking?" He shook his head, as if silently chastising himself. "I can't tell Henry, and you're the only other person here that I trust, Vlad. And now, with my nine-month contract nearing an end, I need help to finish the job. Truth be told, I haven't even started. And I wouldn't normally freak out about it, but the guy that hired me is making threats on my life. And I'm pretty sure he'll deliver, if I don't."

Vlad nodded, as if he understood, but he didn't. Not really.

Joss paused a moment, as if he was searching for the right words. "I didn't move here because of my parents. I came here on my own, because I have a job to do."

Vlad could feel himself leaning forward slightly in anticipation. "What job? What are you talking about?"

Joss held his gaze. "My dad works for this company that moves us all around the world. But the thing is, neither of my parents realizes that I'm the one really working for them. Dad's job is just a cover-up. A cover-up that neither of them is aware of."

Vlad raised an eyebrow and tried to act casual. "For what?"

"For my job. I'm a slayer." Joss nodded matter-of-factly. "A vampire slayer."

No.

His eyes were clear, cold, and honest. And no matter how hard Vlad tried, he couldn't find a joke within them.

No, no, no. Not Joss.

"I was contracted at the beginning of the school year to hunt and kill a vampire that's been lurking around Bathory. It's a private gig, something that the Slayer Society frowns on. Slayers have been banished for taking contracts, which is serious business—if a vampire ever threatens you or your family, you're on your own then. But when I learned that this vampire has been living under cover right in the middle of my cousin's hometown, I couldn't say no, Vlad. You've gotta protect your family." Joss's shoulders relaxed, as if a great weight had been lifted from them. "It was tough convincing my parents that I needed to come stay with Aunt Matilda and Uncle Pete for the year—normally the Society does my convincing for me. It's always tough lying to my mom and dad . . . but with Henry's life on the line, not to mention his brother and parents, there was no way I was going to let this one live."

The knots in Vlad's stomach tightened further until his midsection felt like a solid, heavy mass. "But vampires aren't real."

Joss leaned in close, as if they shared a morbid secret. Strangely, Vlad thought, they did. "Oh yes they are, Vlad. I know. I've killed them."

Vlad swallowed hard and darted his eyes from Joss to the ground and back. "H-how? How did you kill them?"

Joss's tone was frighteningly calm. "Oh, lots of ways. Stake through the heart, mostly. I've dragged a few out into the daylight while they were sleeping. Chopped off a head once. It's pretty brutal, but I believe in the cause behind it, Vlad. If we slayers don't do something about the . . . infestation . . ."

Vlad winced.

". . . the world will be overrun by those things."

Vlad looked at Joss and searched his eyes for a lie. He desperately hoped to find it, but there was none. The boy in front of him was responsible for the death of Vlad's vampire brethren. "How many have you killed?"

"Let's see. . . ." Joss counted on his fingers, then remained quiet for a moment, pondering. "Twenty-three, not counting the two I had help with when I first started out."

Vlad shook his head. "But you don't know anything about them. You don't know if they're evil or not. How do you know they deserve to die?"

Joss pursed his lips. When he spoke, his voice was gruff, as if he were on the brink of tears but fighting them. "I know enough. One killed my sister. I saw it happen. And I'll keep slaying until the world is rid of those monsters."

Monsters. How could Joss call vampires monsters when he was killing them without bothering to get to know anything about them?

"Do you have any idea where the vampire you're hunting is?" Vlad shoved his shaking hands in his front pockets.

Joss's eyes dropped to the ground between Vlad's feet. He seemed very relaxed. Maybe he had no idea he was talking to a *monster.* "Not yet. This one's crafty. And . . . well, I've been distracted, what with the length of the contract, getting to hang out with you and Henry, not to mention Meredith. Listen, you won't tell anyone, will you?"

Vlad thought of telling Otis, but he didn't imagine Otis would react well at all to Vlad's close friend being a slayer. He shook his head, swallowed hard, and dropped his eyes. "What will you do if you find him?"

"It. It's a thing, Vlad. Not a person." Joss squatted down and unzipped his backpack. "I'll do what I'm employed to do—kill it any way I can."

Vlad felt his stomach flip-flop. "Isn't that dangerous?"

Joss cast Vlad a glance that might have been comforting in any other situation. "Relax. The only one who needs to worry about what will happen when I find the vampire, is the vampire."

For some reason, Vlad wasn't comforted by Joss's words.

Joss reached into his backpack and pulled out a large wooden case. He unlocked it with a tarnished, silver key and reached inside, then thrust a small metal object into Vlad's hand. "That's a sterling silver crucifix. Vampires can't go near crosses. And they *hate* silver."

For a second Vlad nearly laughed, but then Joss pulled out a thick, foot-long, wooden stake.

Vlad closed his fist around the silver cross in his hand. He'd never seen a scarier piece of wood.

Joss held it out to him. Vlad squeezed the cross even tighter before handing it over and timidly taking the stake from his friend. "Right between the ribs, and through the heart. But it has to be deep, or they'll fight like crazy."

Vlad swallowed the hard lump that had formed in his throat, "Have you done that . . . for real?"

"Of course I have. These things have to be killed, Vlad. You have no idea what they can do if left unchecked." Joss ran a hand lovingly over a bottle marked GARLIC JUICE. "It's my job to kill them . . . and I like my job."

The last four words that left Joss's lips were almost too much for Vlad to bear. He shook his head, his heart racing in panic. "Joss, this is crazy! These are people we're talking about. Vampires aren't real, you're killing people."

A shadow passed over Joss's features, darker than Vlad had ever seen. "No, Vlad. I'm killing monsters. Monsters that would take a little girl out of her bed and kill her while her big brother watched from the hall, cowering behind the door, too afraid to move or scream."

Vlad stared at his friend in disbelief, lost in the horror of what must have brought Joss to this point. He tried to calm his heart, but it refused to settle its crazy fast beating, so he forcibly relaxed his shoulders and tried to appear calm. Or, at the very least, not like he was the very vampire Joss was hunting. He hefted the weight of the stake in his hand, trying not to picture it in its intended destination.

"Fine. Okay, let's say for a moment that this is all true. What do you do? You just run up and stick this thing into them?"

"That's about it."

Vlad shook his head. No matter what he tried, he couldn't wrap his mind around the sense of it. "No 'Hi, my name is Joss, and I'll be killing you now' or anything like that? Just a stake in the chest, huh?"

Joss shrugged. "That's all it takes. Why waste time talking? That only gives the creature an edge."

"And then what? You just leave them there and hope that they're dead?" Vlad threw up a hand in disgust. A killer. Joss was a killer. And what's worse, Vlad hadn't seen it coming. He wasn't sure who he was madder at: Joss, for being a slayer, or himself, for being stupid enough to befriend a slayer. Vlad made a mental note to amend the friend code: thou shalt not date the girl that thy best friend has a crush on . . . nor shalt thou try sticking thy best friend in the chest with a sharp hunk of wood.

Joss dropped the crucifix back into his case and sighed, as if Vlad was overreacting. "What is the big deal, Vlad? Yes, I leave them there. Once the job is done, it's done. I contact the Society for cleanup and go home."

Vlad dropped his gaze to the ground between them. It was just a few feet but felt worlds apart. "What if you miss?"

In a flash Joss grabbed Vlad's wrist and twisted. Before Vlad knew what happened, Joss had spun Vlad around into a headlock, still holding his wrist. The stake was in Joss's right hand. Vlad didn't even remember letting go of it, yet here it was, being thrust through the air toward the center of Vlad's chest.

Vlad's head swooned, and the color escaped from his face, making him even paler. He'd asked too many questions. Joss had noticed his tattoo. Something. There had to have been something he let slip. Because somehow Joss had realized that Vlad was the only vampire in Bathory. And his friend was about to kill him.

The silver tip of the stake sparkled in the sunlight, hovering less than a quarter of an inch above where Vlad's heart beat forcefully against his chest. His eyes were wide and his breath came in quick, nervous gulps. Joss's whispered voice in his ear confirmed that he wasn't dead. Yet.

"I never miss." Cold determination echoed in his words as Joss lowered the stake and released his friend. Then Joss smiled in bemusement at the look of frozen shock on Vlad's face. "Look, Vlad, I can understand your being uncomfortable. This is a lot to take in all at once. But don't worry. I'm not asking you to stake the thing, just help me find it."

All the betrayal, the terror, the fear that Vlad was feeling boiled over. He shoved Joss back with trembling hands and growled. "What are you doing? You could have seriously hurt me!"

Joss dropped the stake to the ground, stunned. "I was just showing off a little. I thought you'd laugh."

"It's not funny." Vlad shouldered passed him and shot him a furious, terrified glance as he made his way around the corner, heading for home. "And killing people isn't funny either."

Once home, he slammed the door behind him and threw his backpack across the room, just missing Amenti's pudgy body. Both Nelly and the cat looked at him, surprised by his outburst. "Vladimir? Are you okay?"

Vlad ran up the stairs, taking them two at a time. "I'm fine! Just leave me alone, I'm fine!"

He slammed his bedroom door, too, and threw himself onto his bed, trying to shake the image of the stake from his mind.

Through bleary eyes, Vlad glared at the slight glow of his tattoo. A tear escaped his eye and rolled down his cheek. He'd never felt so alone, so frightened, so unbelievably lost and helpless.

That is . . . not since he found his parents dead four years before.

19
A Son's Duty

VLAD BLINKED AT the clock, willing the numbers to change, wanting to get this over with so that he could spend the day feeling a little less sad about what happened four years before. As the numbers switched to 12:01, Vlad bent down and slid on his tennis shoes, tying them haphazardly.

He didn't exactly want to be outside in the middle of the night—especially if Joss was out and about, looking for a vampire to stab in the chest with his wooden stake—but he didn't have much choice in the matter. Some things, like this, were more important than fear.

Not that he wasn't afraid.

On the upside, Vlad was almost positive that Joss hadn't yet realized that he was a vampire, but that didn't stop him from vowing to never invite Joss over for dinner again. With a pause, he tied his other shoe and thought about what it would be like to cut one of his two friends out of his life. How could he? Joss was his friend. A misguided, stake-carrying, threat-to-Vlad's-life friend, but still. Besides, doing anything out of the ordinary might clue Joss in to Vlad's unusual dining habits.

His shoes finally tied, Vlad plucked the Lucis from atop his dresser and crept out of his bedroom into the library. There was a line of light coming from under Nelly's bedroom door. He closed his door behind him and was two steps from the top of the stairs when Amenti darted from the darkness and swatted his ankle. Vlad whispered harshly, "Amenti! Stop that!"

Amenti gave him another good whack with her paw before darting down the stairs. Vlad looked at Nelly's door. There was no way she hadn't heard Amenti's fat body thumping down the stairs like that.

But she didn't open her door.

Vlad crept quietly down the stairs and out the front door. One of these days, Nelly would catch him sneaking out, and he'd be grounded for an eternity.

Outside, the moon had painted the ground blue and the trees an eerie, lifeless gray. It was warm enough for Vlad to forgo his jacket, but by the time he reached downtown,

Vlad wished he'd brought it anyway. There was something oddly comforting about heavy denim against your skin. And comfort was one thing he wasn't finding on his walk to the cemetery.

He hadn't made this walk in an entire year, but he'd repeated this same trip three times now, once a year on the anniversary of the accident. He'd tried coming during the day, but there were always people about. So instead, Vlad chose to pay his respects just a few minutes after midnight, so that he and his parents could spend some time alone, reminiscing about better times, and so that no one would be there to see Vlad cry.

Casting glances over his shoulder every few seconds to be certain neither Eddie Poe nor Joss were following him, Vlad made his way to the edge of town and stopped just in front of the cemetery gates. Short brick walls sat at either side of the entrance, and twisted black wrought iron arched over the dirt path that led inside. At the top of the arch, bold letters identified what lay ahead as LONG ROAD CEMETERY. Vlad had no idea where the name had come from. There wasn't a Long Road in any part of Bathory. But, he thought with a gulp, it certainly was an honest, if not somewhat morbid, name for a place where people bury their dead.

Vlad took a deep breath, brushed his hair from his face with a shaking hand, and stepped forward into the cemetery with his eyes downcast.

Nothing was worse than this pain. Not facing D'Ablo last year. Not being attacked by Jasik. Not being away from Otis. Not running from Joss. Not hiding from Eddie. Nothing.

Halfway up the main path, Vlad paused to look around. The cemetery was overgrown with weeds, and dead ivy and moss hung from the tree trunks. To his left stood a large block-shaped tombstone. Atop it sat a stone woman. In her hand was a wreath of some sort. In the moonlight, she seemed alive, and with a shiver, Vlad waited for her to move.

To his immense relief, she didn't.

To his right was a gravestone that looked like a book, and beside it, one topped with a statue in the shape of a small lamb. Moss had grown over the lamb's tiny nose, and in the moonlit darkness it looked like some weird disease had befallen the animal. Vlad turned his head and saw the large, twisted oak tree that marked where his parents' graves lay. He stepped onto the grass, careful not to cross over the graves. Partly, because it seemed pretty rude to stomp all over someone's remains . . . particularly some-one you hadn't even known. And partly, Vlad gulped, be-cause he'd seen too many movies where the dead would come back to life.

They were just movies, and Vlad knew that. Pure fiction. But nevertheless, he couldn't bring himself to cross over the graves, for fear someone . . . or something . . . would rip through the earth and latch onto his ankle.

He took slow, tentative steps toward the tree, sweeping the stones with his eyes. At the base of the tree he saw it: his parents' tombstone.

It was a small stone, tasteful, simple. At each of the top corners ivy leaves were engraved, pointing down to the inscription: **IN HONORED MEMORY OF TOMAS AND MELLINA TOD.** Below that were their birthdates, the date they were married, and the date of their demise. At the very bottom was a simple inscription, one that Nelly was brave enough to choose for the stone when Vlad had not been: **WE'LL MISS YOU.**

Vlad knelt before the stone, stretching his hand out to brush away the dead leaves and dirt that had accumulated over the past year. He dropped his gaze to the ground and tried hard not to think about the last time he saw them, or the fact that their bodies were lying several feet below in the cold, hallowed ground. When he looked back at the stone, he read the inscription again and cleared his throat. "People keep saying it'll get easier."

Hot tears welled in Vlad's eyes. He brushed them away with the back of his hand and took a slow, deep breath. "People are stupid."

Vlad bit his bottom lip gently and shook his head. "It never gets easier, missing you. And sometimes I wonder if it ever will."

A small animal raced out of the nearby woods and paused to chew some freshly sprouted clover. Vlad watched it for a moment in deep thought. He sat that way, mulling over the memory of the day he'd found them dead, going over all of the details he could recall of that horrible moment and the days after, until his feet had finally tingled with numbness, forcing him to sit on the ground. After what seemed like forever, he stood and brushed the grass and dirt from his jeans. He ran a caring hand over the top of their stone and let the tears come. They rolled down his cheeks in streams. "I'm sorry. I'm sorry I turned off your alarm. If there was any way I could take it back, I would."

His shoulders shook as his silent tears gave way to painful sobs. After a while, he dried his face with his sleeve and took a few breaths, squelching his sadness for the moment. When he'd calmed himself down, he whispered, "But I can't. And I have to learn to live with that."

Once he left the cemetery, he walked straight home, all the while trying not to think about his parents anymore. Instead he focused on Joss. Clearly Vlad had to do something about his slayer friend. And avoiding Joss or trusting him with his deepest secret was out of the question, so his options were pretty limited. It came down to two choices, and neither seemed very appealing.

He could either stand up to Joss, attacking first, gaining the upper hand—and, with luck, scaring Joss off for good, or he could manipulate Joss by assisting in his search for the vampire of Bathory. A few wrong turns initiated by Vlad might just be the trick to throw Joss off the trail. But the idea of betraying a friend left a terrible taste in Vlad's mouth. What was that quote about keeping your friends close and your enemies closer? It didn't matter. It was good advice, all the same.

Still, when it came down to Vlad's life or his friendship with Joss, the choice was pretty easy to make.

Eddie . . . well, Eddie was another complication altogether.

Vlad moved between some houses and came out across the street from his old house—the one he'd lived in from the time he was a baby until he moved out to live with Nelly. He glanced back over his shoulder, completely baffled as to how he'd ended up here when he was sure he'd been heading straight home.

The house looked so hollow in the moonlight, alone, empty. Vlad wondered if he'd ever live there again. The house was legally his, the deed held by Nelly for him until he turned eighteen. Sometimes he daydreamed about fixing up the house and living there with a family of his own someday.

Sometimes he wished it would just shrivel up and disappear, folding in on itself until it was no more. But then he'd remember some small detail about his parents, and the guilty tears would come, washing away all of those dark wishes and reminding him that there was a reason the house still stood. It was a symbol of his family—and even death couldn't take them from him.

Across the street, a man was walking toward Vlad's old house. The man stopped and turned back, as if scanning the shadows for any sign he was being watched. Vlad ducked behind a tree, waited for a few seconds, and then dared a glance.

Vlad knew that man. It was Jasik—the vampire who'd bitten him.

Jasik stepped up to the porch, opened the door, and went inside. The door had only just latched before Vlad bolted across the street. His heart was hammering away at his ribs, but something deeper pushed him on, something darker. He had to see what Jasik was doing inside his old house, just had to.

Because he'd hoped that his last encounter with Jasik would be the extent of their encounters, and clearly, it wasn't.

Vlad crept around back and peeked through the dining room window. The house looked empty. Jasik must have gone upstairs.

With a trembling hand, Vlad opened the back door and closed it behind him. Every horror movie he'd ever seen said that this was a bad idea, but he crept forward anyway and ignored the pounding within his chest. The entire house smelled like ash and soot, even though the fire that had taken his parents from him had been confined to their bedroom alone. Vlad tried hard not to look at anything but his feet, but he failed miserably. His dad's briefcase was on the dining room table, netted down with a layer of cobwebs and dust. Inside, everything would be in pristine condition, untouched, despite the years. Like going back in time—the same way Vlad went back in time every time he entered his old house.

Vlad padded silently across the wood floors and up the stairs, where he listened closely for a hint of Jasik's movements. Down the hall, in his father's study, he could hear Jasik moving around. It sounded as if he was opening and closing the drawers of the desk. Vlad snuck into the hall for a closer look.

Jasik stepped abruptly out of the study and moved down the hall to the master bedroom.

Vlad lurched to a halt and got ready to bolt, certain he'd been spotted. To his amazement, Jasik entered the bedroom without as much as a glance at him. He let out a sigh and took a few careful steps down the hall, then hid in one of the darker corners, beside a large grandfather clock. The door to the bedroom was open, so Vlad watched Jasik dart about, dropping things that he must have brought with him into a leather satchel. Jasik cursed loudly, but it wasn't in English. The tone alone was enough to let Vlad know he was swearing. Vlad wondered if the language he spoke might be Elysian code. But it didn't matter. What mattered was *why* Jasik had sworn.

Jasik stomped about the room, still grumbling under his breath in that strange language. He ran his fingers along various sections of the wall, and then returned to throwing his belongings angrily into his bag. The sight might have been comical if a vial of blood weren't poking out from Jasik's shirt pocket—a vial he was pretty sure he'd seen Jasik spit his blood into after attacking him in front of Nelly's house three months before. Vlad thought of pushing into Jasik's thoughts, but he was almost certain that would clue Jasik in to his presence. If Vlad could tell when Otis was trying to read his mind, surely Jasik would know if Vlad dared to try.

Jasik slipped his jacket back on and picked up his bag. He paused for a moment, as if listening.

Vlad cupped his hand over his mouth and kept very, very still.

Jasik turned toward the hall, slowly.

Vlad stiffened. He'd been caught. There was no way Jasik would let him leave now, with the rest of his blood intact. Still, he didn't move, didn't breathe.

Jasik stepped into the hall and paused near the large clock. Notes from Beethoven's Fifth Symphony erupted from his pocket. He withdrew a cell phone and placed it to his ear. "Yes?"

A pause as he listened.

"I have the boy's blood, but not the Lucis. I'm headed back to Elysia now." He turned away from Vlad and lowered his voice. "It hardly matters. From what I read in Tomas's notes, it's not even in Bathory."

A pause, then a sigh. "I had thought Tomas's son might lead me to it, but clearly he has no knowledge of it, so there's no need to prolong his life any further."

Jasik mumbled something that Vlad couldn't hear and then pushed a button and shoved the phone back into his pocket. With his bag in hand, he descended the stairs without a word. Vlad listened and heard the front door slam shut. He breathed a huge sigh of relief.

Only temporary relief, though. Because Jasik had been talking about killing him.

After a brief search in the study, Vlad paused just outside his parents' bedroom door. He hadn't been in there since the day they died. But if Jasik had left some sort of clue behind as to who he was and what he wanted with Vlad's blood, then now wasn't the time for painful memories. Vlad stepped inside and forced his eyes about the charred remains of the room.

Silvery moonlight was peeking through the boards on the room's only window. It provided just enough light for Vlad to have a decent view of his parents' room and the remains of the bed they'd once slept in.

He saw nothing at all that seemed out of place or unusual, but something was definitely going on with Jasik, and Vlad needed to know what it was.

Even if it meant taking a trip into the heart of Elysia without Otis there to guide or protect him.

20
An Enemy Revealed

VLAD FOCUSED ON the center of his body and willed his feet to leave the ground. Within seconds, he was hovering in front of Henry's bedroom window.

Henry was on his bed, snoring loudly.

Vlad tapped the glass. "Henry."

Henry snorted and rolled onto his side. His hand was dangling off the side of the bed.

Vlad knocked a knuckle hard against the window frame. "Henry, wake up!"

Henry sat up at once and rubbed his eyes. After a brief look around, he saw Vlad out the window and staggered over, stifling a yawn. "Hey . . . I've seen this movie. Vampire floats up to the window. Guy invites him in. Vampire sucks the guy's blood, and he turns into one of the vampire's minions."

Henry opened the window and leaned on the window-sill, offering a weary but bemused smile to Vlad. "No way am I inviting you in."

Vlad rolled his eyes. "Dude, just move over so I can come inside."

Henry stepped back and stretched his arms overhead, suppressing another yawn. "Ya know, some of us sleep when the sun goes down."

Vlad climbed through the window. "Yeah, but some of us are out uncovering schemes that involve Elysia . . . and my blood."

Henry's smile faded. "What do you mean?"

Vlad opened one of Henry's dresser drawers and threw a T-shirt to Henry. "That vampire that bit me? He spit some of my blood into a vial he had with him. And tonight I caught him at my old house. I need a ride to Stokerton, so I can find out why."

Henry's jaw almost hit the floor.

Vlad picked up a pair of jeans and tossed them at him. "Are you going to help me or not?"

Henry stepped into his jeans and shook his head. "Have you forgotten neither of us knows how to operate a motor vehicle?"

Vlad was on his knees, digging out Henry's shoes from under the bed. Successful in his search, he tossed them at Henry's feet. "I realize that, but Greg can drive."

Henry sighed and slipped his shoes on. "And you woke me up because. . . ?"

Vlad sighed. "I need you to keep him busy while I go into Elysia."

"Alone?! Are you nuts? You shouldn't go near that place without Otis."

"I don't have much choice, Henry. Otis might not even be getting my letters, and whatever this guy is up to, he's up to it now." Vlad gave him a pleading look. "Just wake your brother up and ask him, okay?"

Henry slipped the shirt on over his head and stepped quietly across the hall. He entered Greg's room, and after a mumbled conversation, a groggy Greg followed Henry back across the hall. Greg scratched his head. His hair was sticking up this way and that. "What's goin' on, Vlad? Henry says you need me to drive you into Stokerton or somethin'."

Behind him, Henry shrugged at Vlad. No help there.

Vlad cleared his throat. "Yeah, I do, Greg. Could you?"

"Well, not without a good reason." Greg folded his arms in front of him. "So . . . what's the reason?"

Vlad looked at Henry, who shrugged, wide-eyed. Vlad said, "Twenty bucks."

Greg grinned. "Good reason. Make it thirty, and you've got a deal."

Vlad pulled two bills out of his wallet and handed them to Greg.

Greg glanced over his shoulder and lowered his voice even further. "Meet me outside in ten minutes. I just gotta get dressed first. And be quiet—if Mom and Dad catch us, we're all in trouble."

Minutes later, they were in the car and on their way to Stokerton. Greg asked all sorts of obnoxious questions about the girl that Vlad was sneaking out to see—it had to be a girl, Greg reasoned. Thirty bucks and two hours in the car would only really be worth it if there was a girl involved. For the most part, Vlad ignored him. Henry occasionally distracted his brother with questions about the upcoming season for the Bathory Bats. Finally, they pulled into Stokerton, and Vlad directed Greg down the streets until they came to a stop in front of the thirteen-story office building that Vlad had revisited in his sleep many times.

"Just wait here." Vlad opened the car door and stepped out, ignoring a worried glance from Henry. The last time they'd been here, Henry had watched as Vlad defended himself to the death against D'Ablo. He walked around the corner to the hole in the wall near the Dumpster and slid inside.

The tunnel was just as cramped and filthy as he remembered. Vlad crawled through it until he reached the metal shaft that led down to the furnace. He squeezed his way upward and popped open the grate that led into one of Elysia's holding cells. As he lifted himself into the cell, it occurred to Vlad what a stupid venture this would have been if the cell door was locked. Luckily it wasn't, and it slid open with ease.

Vlad made his way down the hall, and after a brief listen at the door, he stepped into the empty council room. He crossed the room and, straining his memory to recall which way the elevator was, opened another door a crack.

Jasik passed the door and stepped into the elevator.

Vlad watched the numbers climb to thirteen and stop. He moved to the elevator and pressed the up button. Lucky for him, the building was mostly empty. When the elevator came, he stepped inside. He touched his hand to a glyph in the wood, just as his uncle had done a year before, and the panel flipped open to reveal a second set of buttons. Vlad pressed thirteen and waited.

When the doors opened, Vlad stepped out and looked around for Jasik. At the end of the hall two gloss black double doors stood open. Golden light poured from within. Vlad moved closer, sliding silently along the wall, and listened.

"So?" A pause, then a small gasp. "Excellent, Jasik. And the boy?"

"Unharmed, as you instructed."

Vlad held his breath and peered around the corner. Jasik was sitting in a chair near the large, black desk. The other man was facing the window, clutching the vial of Vlad's blood in his hand. Neither had noticed Vlad's presence.

The man by the window straightened his shoulders but didn't tear his gaze from the view outside. "Good. I want to be there to witness his demise."

Jasik raised an eyebrow. "I thought you believed him to be the Pravus."

The man grew quiet before answering in a soft, almost tranquil tone. "I do. But I also must prove my belief to the world, remove all doubt. And to do so, I must take his life."

Jasik snorted. "And violate the highest law?"

"Not at all. I've made other arrangements. You don't expect them to give me back my presidency after I've killed one of our own kind, do you?"

"Of course not." Jasik's tone said that he wasn't exactly sure whether the man was a lawbreaker or not. "So what if you're right, and he manages to survive death?"

The man turned around slowly. His black gloves shimmered in the low light. His long coat billowed as he moved. Black leather pants clung to his legs, but his chest was bare beneath the coat. Vlad gasped at the large hole in the man's stomach. He had to place his hand over his mouth to contain the scream that threatened to boil up from within him.

D'Ablo smirked at Jasik and then held the vial of blood up to the light. "Then I want to be there to welcome him on bended knee."

Vlad ducked out of sight, hand still clamped over his mouth. D'Ablo was alive. How was this possible? He remembered everything. The dark alley. The terrifying uncertainty as he pointed the Lucis at D'Ablo and ran his thumb over the glyph. Even Otis had said that they should just let him die. And die he had, right before Vlad's eyes.

And yet the man in the next room was D'Ablo, with the same, though somewhat smaller, hole in his stomach.

Vlad peeked around the corner again. D'Ablo had uncapped the vial of Vlad's blood and was sniffing the air above it, as a human would a fine wine. He lifted it a bit in a toasting gesture and opened his mouth as he tilted the open vial. Liquid rubies spilled from the container to D'Ablo's tongue.

D'Ablo held the liquid in his mouth for a moment, apparently savoring the flavor. His head was tilted back slightly, his eyes closed. Vlad watched D'Ablo's Adam's apple rise and fall as his blood slipped down his throat.

The office was completely silent, as if the very air feared to move. Vlad's heart drummed out a quick rhythm, pumping blood through his limbs, but his body was numb. After what seemed like an eternity, the silence was broken.

The sound was small at first, like an army of spiders moving in from far away. But it grew quickly, as if that army had started to run. Vlad watched, mesmerized, terrified, as the hole in D'Ablo's center began to move, to flex around the edges. A strand of tissue shot across the diameter of the hole, followed by another. And another. Forming a strange web of flesh—accompanied by the now deafening spider sounds. The hole through D'Ablo was closing.

Once it began, it moved very quickly. Strands gave way to muscle. Muscle joined to form organs. Organs were covered with skin. The spider sounds died down, and D'Ablo was whole again.

With carefully quiet movements, Vlad stood and slinked back down the hallway, almost knocking over a planter on his way out. It wobbled, but he steadied it and continued down the hall.

Things couldn't get much worse. His uncle was missing in action, one of his best friends wanted to kill him, and that was just the beginning.

D'Ablo was still alive.

And he still wanted Vlad dead.

Vlad took the elevator to the first floor and staggered out the front door. He opened the door to the car and slid in beside Henry.

Henry wrinkled his brow. "Everything okay?"

Vlad shook his head once and then turned to the window, hoping Henry would take a hint and lay off. There was only one person Vlad wanted to talk to about D'Ablo's return—and he wasn't answering Vlad's letters.

In the driver's seat Greg chuckled. "Women. They'll steer you wrong every time, Vlad."

The ride home was silent, and but for the occasional nudge and worried glance from Henry, Vlad was left alone with his thoughts.

He had no idea how D'Ablo had survived having the Lucis shoot a giant hole through his stomach. Nor did he have any clue as to how Otis could have not known that D'Ablo survived. And what right did Vlad have to feel sickened by the sight of a vampire feeding on his blood, when he feasted on human blood every day? Sometimes he felt like such a hypocrite.

Vlad slumped down in his seat and watched the lights of the city disappear. Soon there was nothing to see but twinkling stars and wide-open, dark places. When people had mentioned how difficult his freshman year would be, he had no idea how right they would be. Of course, they didn't have a vindictive, evil monster coming back from the dead and chasing after them, or a slayer who just happened to be one of his best friends.

Vlad sighed. What was he going to do about Joss? He couldn't tell Joss the truth, couldn't risk exposing himself—not if Joss was carrying a wooden stake and garlic around with him. And now, with D'Ablo making plans to watch Vlad die . . . Bathory was about to become an enormously uncomfortable place for Vlad to live.

Maybe he'd luck out and Joss would stumble upon D'Ablo before D'Ablo had a chance to reach Vlad.

Vlad smirked at the thought, and then furrowed his brow.

That wasn't such a bad idea.

If Joss killed D'Ablo, it would fix everything. Joss would be satisfied in his hunt for the local vampire. D'Ablo wouldn't be around to try to take Vlad's life—presuming of course that D'Ablo stayed dead this time. And Vlad wouldn't have to reveal his secret to Joss at all. All of his problems would be solved, without the intervention of Otis.

Greg turned on the radio. The Killers were on, singing a slow tune about how everything would be all right. Vlad leaned against the door and stared up at the stars, wishing against all odds that they were right.

21
ET TU, JOSS?

VLAD PANTED FOR AIR and cast Mr. Hunjo a pleading look of desperation, but the gym teacher had clearly lost his ability to pity a dying boy, if indeed he'd ever had it. He grunted, "Keep it moving, Tod. Pick those knees up."

Vlad rounded the corner but didn't pick up his knees. Any farther up and he'd be kneeing himself in the jaw.

Joss ran up beside him. He was barely breaking a sweat. "You okay, Vlad?"

Vlad panted between words. "No . . . dying . . . Hunjo . . . jerk . . ." If stakes and garlic were the top two things that could kill a vampire, ninth grade gym was a close third.

Joss kept stride with Vlad until they were getting ready to pass Mr. Hunjo again and then said, "No problem." He took off at a sprint, and before Vlad could raise an exhausted eyebrow, Joss tumbled forward onto the track.

Vlad hurried over to him and helped him up. "What are you doing? Are you okay?"

Joss winced as he put weight on his left leg. "My knee."

Mr. Hunjo bellowed, "Tod! Help McMillan to the nurse's office."

Joss threw his arm around Vlad's shoulder, and Vlad helped him limp out into the hallway. As soon as the gym door closed, Joss let go of Vlad and started walking normally. Vlad smirked. "You're a quick healer."

Joss shrugged. "Hey, I was saving us both. You from death, me from boredom."

Vlad took a deep breath. He was ready. He'd gone over his plan for two solid weeks and could find no holes. It was going to work. "Listen, Joss, can I talk to you for a second?"

Joss held the bathroom door open for Vlad. He looked very tired—probably due to late-night monster hunting in the two weeks since his confession. "Sure thing. Step into my office."

Vlad chewed his bottom lip thoughtfully. "Are we cool? I mean, after I ran off the other day, I thought I might have messed up the trust we've been building."

Joss smiled. "We're cool, Vlad. It's no big deal. I just didn't want you thinking I was some nutcase, going around killing people."

"I don't. Well, you know, what you told me a few weeks ago about vampires and slayers had me convinced you belonged in the loony bin. But after last night . . . I kind of believe you."

Joss's eyes grew wide, his tone serious. "Why? What happened last night?"

Vlad cleared his throat and darted his eyes purposely around. "I think I saw a vampire."

Joss leaned closer. "You think or you know? We have to be certain, Vlad."

"It was. He had fangs and was really pale." Vlad nodded, feeling the weight of his heavy lunch in his stomach like a ball of lead.

Joss nodded. "Sounds like a bloodsucker to me."

Vlad swallowed hard. "He attacked me and then jumped in a car and drove off toward Stokerton."

A terrible expression crossed Joss's face—a weird mixture of curiosity, surprise, and shrewdness. Vlad was ready to experience the flight portion of the fight-or-flight response they'd just discussed in biology, when Joss said, "He attacked you and you got away?"

Vlad nodded, hoping the glint in Joss's eyes wasn't suspicion.

Joss smiled. "I'm impressed. You might have what it takes to be a slayer after all."

The bell rang. Vlad forced a smile and led Joss out the door and down the hall to the locker room to change. "So what are you going to do?"

Joss thought for a second, then said, "Well, you said he drove toward Stokerton. I'll get my aunt to drop us off tomorrow afternoon and we'll go hunting."

Vlad looked at Joss. He wasn't sure he could stomach seeing a fellow vampire murdered, even if it was D'Ablo. "We?"

"Well, yeah, Vlad. I mean, you know what it looks like. Besides, I want to show you how it's done. Not often do I get to show off my moves." Joss winked at him, and Vlad felt immediately sick to his stomach. "I'll come over after dinner tonight and we can go over the details."

Vlad nodded without speaking. As he opened the locker room door, Joss limped his way inside.

Vlad pushed the thought of watching another vampire die out of his mind for the rest of the day. When he got home that afternoon, the house was quiet—Nelly was working overtime at the hospital again. Vlad left his backpack on the floor and went upstairs. He searched the shelves of the library but found next to nothing on vampire slayers. Apparently the only myths around them had been captured by Bram Stoker. Vlad snorted. Where was Buffy's wisdom when you needed it?

He stepped into his bedroom and sat on the bed. His limbs were full of nervous energy. In just twenty-four hours, he'd be confronting D'Ablo again.

No, Vlad. Stop thinking that way.

Joss would be confronting D'Ablo. Vlad would be cowering behind a Dumpster and hoping that D'Ablo didn't see him.

You'd think that having managed to blow a hole through an attacking vampire would make a guy more confident, but the fact of the matter was that last year's events had scared the crap out of Vlad. He didn't enjoy killing. He didn't enjoy hurting anyone. Even if the person he was hurting was out for his blood.

He went downstairs to the kitchen and grabbed a bag of blood from the freezer. Tearing it open with his teeth, he poured the sticky sweet liquid into a coffee mug, and then sat it in the microwave and pressed the one-minute button. After it beeped, Vlad pulled the cup out and blew the steam away before taking a healthy gulp.

Nelly wouldn't be home for another few hours. He had no real idea of when Joss would show up, but Vlad bet that he'd be along shortly after Nelly. So with nothing to do but algebra, Vlad settled down in front of the television with controller in hand. He'd take out his recent frustrations on the menacing alien king.

Several hours later, after having lost to the computer four times, Vlad tossed his controller on the floor and ran a stressed hand through his hair. Nelly walked through the door, carrying a bag of groceries. "Evening, dear. How was your day?"

Vlad bit his bottom lip in contemplation. On the one hand, he wanted to spill everything about Joss and D'Ablo to someone who might be able to protect him in some small way. On the other hand, he didn't want to get Nelly involved. D'Ablo was dangerous—too dangerous for Vlad's guardian. "Pretty uneventful."

Out the front window, Vlad saw Joss step onto the porch. A moment later, he rang the bell. Vlad slipped his sneakers on.

"Nelly, I'm going to hang out with Joss for a while. I'll be back in about an hour." Before she could answer, he was out the door, and he and Joss were walking down the street.

Joss seemed distant, distracted. By the time the conversation rolled around to vampires, they were headed toward the edge of town.

Vlad eyed Joss's backpack warily. "So, where are we going?"

"For a walk. I have an unexpected errand to run." Joss pulled his shoulders back. Vlad was sure he saw Joss strut a little. "You'll have to stay out of sight during my rendezvous, but afterward I'll run through some maneuvers with you for tomorrow."

They walked past the Barker farm and into the woods on the very edge of what the map called Bathory. Up the hill some, the trees broke into a clearing. At the center of it stood a man dressed in black.

D'Ablo.

Vlad froze. His heart picked up its pace and thumped hard enough against his ribs to propel him forward a step. Gripping Joss by the arm, Vlad tugged him behind a nearby tree and tried hard to think of a quick way to escape without being noticed. They could slip back down the hill without a word, but that would require Joss's total, unquestioning silence—something Vlad wasn't sure he could get without mind control or a really, really good explanation. Unless, of course, he put plan Solve All Vlad's Problems into effect a little early.

Joss yanked his arm away. "What are you doing?"

Vlad peeked around the tree at D'Ablo and back at Joss. A giant lump had formed in his throat, making it difficult to force out words. "You see that guy out there? He's the vampire."

Joss rolled his eyes and stepped from behind the tree. To Vlad's horror, Joss's movement caught D'Ablo's attention. Vlad yanked on Joss's arm again, but Joss shook him off. "Vlad, no offense, but I'm a slayer. I think I know how to spot a vampire. Besides . . ."

Joss waved to D'Ablo, who nodded in return.

Vlad looked from Joss to D'Ablo and back. Something was very wrong.

Joss offered a comforting smile to Vlad. "He's the guy who hired me."

Vlad looked back at D'Ablo, who was smiling calmly. A slight snarl raised on D'Ablo's lip, so subtly that Vlad was certain Joss hadn't seen it. He glanced at Joss—poor, unsuspecting Joss—and knew that if he didn't do something, Joss would be D'Ablo's next meal. He took a deep breath and stepped out into the clearing, keeping his eyes on D'Ablo the whole time. "You hired a slayer?"

D'Ablo's lips curled into a cruel smile. "I had no choice. Believe me, boy, I would relish taking my revenge directly. But you see, our little brush last year left me scarred, which stole the council presidency from me. Last year, killing you would have been Elysian justice. This year, as the council now insists that if you are indeed a vampire, you are to be interviewed and then tried, a justified murder of you by my own hand without the council's consent would be illegal. If I ever hope to regain my presidency—and I will; that force is already in motion—I can't go breaking the highest law by killing my own kind. That would condemn me to death—assuming the council ever consents that you are one of us. And I rather enjoy living."

Vlad cast a glance at D'Ablo's stomach, remembering the hole and the sound of a thousand spiders as he'd watched it heal closed. "So the Lucis . . ."

"Yes. It's the epitome of weapons against vampirekind. I was fortunate. Had you actually known what it was capable of last year, and had you aimed any higher, we might not be engaging in this conversation. Of course, if it weren't for your Pravus blood, I'd be scarred and wounded for life. Unwhole." D'Ablo's eyes were haunted for a moment. Then his features lightened, and the corner of his mouth rose in bemusement. His eyes sparkled some in the moonlight. "It seems I owe you some gratitude. The blood of the Pravus has enormous healing capabilities."

"I'm not the Pravus." Vlad's voice wavered—even he didn't believe his words anymore.

D'Ablo clucked his tongue. "Oh, I believe that you are. Surely even you can't deny the possibility."

Vlad's heart sank. It was possible, no matter how much he wanted to deny that possibility.

Vlad weighed his words carefully before wetting his lips and speaking. "If I am the Pravus, that means I'm a vampire. So, why aren't you taking me in to be interviewed and tried for my crimes? Or do you plan to capture me and harvest my blood?"

D'Ablo raised a sharp eyebrow. "No. I have no plans to capture you. I cannot kill you by my hand, but by a wayward slayer's hand, I can. It's really quite simple. I must prove that you are the Pravus, and the only way to do that is to do what I can to kill you. You have what I want, and trying you before the council won't give it to me."

With a nervous shudder, Vlad met D'Ablo's eyes. "What do you want?"

Taking a step closer, a wicked smile crossed D'Ablo's face. "Ultimately? To take your place as the Pravus. But for that, I require three specific items . . . and, of course, your life."

Vlad took a step back but didn't speak. His heart had become eerily quiet, as if by not making any sudden movements, it could escape being ripped from his chest.

D'Ablo chuckled, low and metallic. "If you are the Pravus, as I believe that you are, I will require your life to perform a very special ritual. First, of course, I must locate the precise instructions for performing the last part of the ritual. If you manage to survive tonight, I'll be back to collect you. After all, I'm ill equipped to care for a prisoner until the time when I discover the passage I'm seeking. It may take years. Though I hope it will be much sooner.

"It's not a proven method, of course. But texts that I've studied over the years insist that once the ceremony is complete, I will be the one to reign over vampirekind and to enslave the human race, and you . . . you shall rot." He paused then, as if letting the enormity of Vlad's situation sink in. Then he offered a nod to Joss, who'd been standing strangely quiet this entire time. Almost, Vlad thought curiously, as if he were spellbound. "Our dear slayer here will try to take your life in a moment. If you live, we will have proven beyond all doubt that you are the Pravus. And the naysayers, the millions of vampires who insist that the prophecy is nothing but a fairy tale, will at last become believers. Believers who will be forced to follow me as the new Pravus once I complete a ceremony that is already in the works. They will obey my law, my customs, without question. No more councils, paperwork, difficulty. I will rule over all vampires with an iron fist." His chest rose and fell quickly in excited breaths. Then, as if snapping out of his delusion, D'Ablo said, "If you die, I was wrong about you—a shame, really, but nothing I'll feel condolences for. Either way, it is a win-win situation for me."

Vlad's mouth was completely dry. Even if he survived tonight, D'Ablo was determined to kill him. He had to end this. Running away wasn't an option. Unless he ran long enough to get Otis's help. But that would require an escape plan. And not just from D'Ablo.

His eyes flitted to Jasik and back. Jasik was standing behind D'Ablo.

Running his hand over his pocket, Vlad relaxed some. He still had the Lucis. He could end this all with a touch . . . and good aim. But he needed time, and distance. Slowly, he lifted his foot from the ground and took a step back. "Otis said that you and my dad were friends."

"We were. But Tomas is dead. What greater gift can I give him than to send him his son?"

"How'd you know Joss would bring me here?" Vlad risked another step. Two more and he'd have the distance he needed to put a big hole right through D'Ablo and his sordid plan. As for what to do about Jasik and Joss after that happened . . . he had no idea.

"You act as if planting suggestions in the mind of a human is complicated." A smirk danced on D'Ablo's lips. "It isn't. Neither is blocking from his thoughts the fact that Jasik and I are of the same species that he is hunting, or keeping him in check during our little reunion."

"So why did you wait all year long? It's not like Bathory is a metropolis. I'm not exactly hard to find." Another step. One more and D'Ablo's holier-than-thou attitude would be justified.

"Though you are of the utmost importance, *sire*"—Vlad thought he detected a note of sarcasm, but it was difficult to tell—"being fully healed is not enough to regain my presidency. However, if I take the council nine months of logs documenting the procedures and locations of the Slayer Society, the council will quickly warm to me, I assure you."

Vlad snorted and slowly lifted his foot. "Don't you find any irony in a vampire sucking up?"

D'Ablo's pinched expression oozed impatience. "Enough of this. It's time to face your destiny, Vladimir Tod."

Vlad reached into his pocket and withdrew the Lucis. He held it up and pointed it straight at D'Ablo's chest. "Not so fast."

D'Ablo parted his lips and laughed. His laughter was low, strange, and chilling, as if he knew something that Vlad didn't.

Vlad ran his thumb across the glyph at the end of the Lucis and waited for a bright white light to shoot out of the other end. But nothing happened.

Vlad tried again, but the Lucis refused to respond. It was as if the tool were broken.

D'Ablo's laughter grew louder still. "You should have listened to your uncle's warning concerning taking the Lucis with you everywhere, Vladimir. For all you know, some rogue vampire could easily steal his way into your room one day while you were studying human biology, and pluck it from atop your dresser. And if he was cunning, he might replace the real Lucis with a fake one so as not to raise suspicions."

Jasik grinned broadly and held up the Lucis, the real Lucis. Vlad's heart raced as he dropped the fake Lucis to the ground. A wave of panic threatened to sweep over him. He reached over, placed his hand on Joss's shoulder, and whispered, "Joss, do you have that case in your backpack still?"

But Joss wasn't listening. He had his eyes locked on Vlad's wrist.

Vlad pulled his hand back. His tattoo was glowing brightly. He opened his mouth, then closed it again, unsure what he could say to explain the strange, glowing mark. His heart had sunk deep into his stomach and had taken his voice box with it.

"All this time you pretended to be my friend and you were one of them, Vlad?" Joss wrenched his shoulder away, suddenly free of whatever spell had held him still and silent. He pinched the zipper pull on his bag and tugged, exposing the case within. Carefully, almost lovingly, he withdrew the wooden box and unlocked it, flipping open the lid. "I don't want to do this. You have no idea how difficult your death will be to explain to Henry."

Vlad watched Joss closely, hardly able to believe one of his closest friends was about to make an attempt on his life. He formed apology after apology in his mind, but none sounded anywhere near sensible. What was he apologizing for? Joss was the one in the wrong here. He almost said precisely that, but there was something else that kept his attention—the fact that Joss seemed completely oblivious to Jasik and D'Ablo now . . . almost like he was being made to focus only on Vlad and the task at hand.

Behind Joss, Jasik handed D'Ablo the Lucis. D'Ablo smiled and slipped it in an inside pocket of his jacket. Under his breath, D'Ablo said, "That's two of the three items we require. And the third we'll collect soon enough."

Joss withdrew the wooden stake, and in the glint of silver at its tip, Vlad found his voice. "Henry knows."

Joss's brow creased. "What? What do you mean? You told him I'm a slayer?"

Vlad shook his head slowly. He kept darting his eyes between the vampires behind Joss and the weapon in Joss's hand. "He knows I'm a vampire. He's known since we were eight. He keeps my secret for me—Nelly does, too. So you see, no one in Bathory was ever in danger from me. I drink donated blood, and never from the source. I know you think that vampires are evil monsters, but I'm not. I'm different."

Joss cast Vlad a doubtful glance. "You're lying. Henry tells me everything."

"Not this." Behind Joss, D'Ablo whispered something to Jasik, who nodded. Vlad pushed with his mind until he had a headache, but couldn't read either of their thoughts. Pushing as hard as he could, he thought to Otis, *Help me, Uncle Otis! D'Ablo is alive! Do you hear me? He's alive and trying to kill me!*

But there was no answer.

He took a very slow step back and wondered if he could outrun them all. "If you kill me, Henry will find out you're a slayer. Your whole family will find out."

Joss stepped closer, matching Vlad's pace. The kindness had gone out of his eyes. "I can live with that." He hefted the weight of the stake in his hand and raised an eyebrow at Vlad. "But you won't."

Joss broke into a run. He thrust the stake forward, its tip gleaming in the moonlight. Vlad dodged it and sprinted across the clearing. He turned back to Joss and held his hands up. "You don't have to do this, Joss. Think about it. Who's the real monster here? It's D'Ablo that set this up. You and I are friends."

Vlad locked eyes with Joss and pushed hard with his mind. With a dizzying rush of blood to the head, he slipped into Joss's thoughts with ease.

Joss gripped the stake in his hands. Friends or not, he had to do it, had to kill Vlad to save Cecile. She was dead, yes, but every time he took another vampire down, he could feel her soul growing just a little lighter. He was easing her pain now in a way he'd been unable to in her final moments.

But wait . . . Vlad was his friend. How could he take the life of a boy he'd reached out to, who understood what it was like to lose someone close to you? He couldn't . . . he couldn't.

Vlad pulled out of his thoughts and waited, hoping that this would all be over soon. Or at the very least, that he and Joss would be on the same side, facing D'Ablo and Jasik as a team.

Joss paused for a moment, clearly mulling over the thoughts Vlad had placed in his mind. Then, shaking his head, he retrieved a vial from the case with his free hand and opened the lid. His eyes were clear, cold. "You're a bloodsucker. And I can't let you live."

Vlad watched the vial in horror. Garlic juice. Great.

He pushed again, once more invading Joss's thoughts, trying to gain control.

A searing pain shot through Joss's head, as if his brain was the subject of a tug-of-war. He focused on the task at hand, which flitted through his mind in one single, rambling direction. *KillVladKillVladKillVladKillVlad* . . .

He clutched the bottle in his hand and stood, his eyes on the beast, the monster that was so like the creature who'd taken his Cecile. *KillVladKillVladKillVladKillVlad . . .*

Monster? This was Vlad. One of his two only friends. He should at least talk to him, maybe help him fend off these other jerks before he did something stupid.

Vlad pulled out of Joss's mind again and looked at D'Ablo, certain he'd been controlling Joss's thoughts. He cleared his throat, unsure if his skill at mind control would be enough to deter the slayer, and returned his gaze to the small glass bottle. "You'd kill me just because some guy told you to? Some guy who is, by the way, a vampire."

Joss pursed his lips and glared, tightening his grip on both the vial and the stake. "I'm doing this because it's the right thing to do. I could give a damn what he is. This goes beyond a sense of duty, Vlad. Now it's personal."

Vlad's jaw dropped. "You've lost it."

Joss drew his arm back and whipped the vial through the air, spilling its contents in a shower of small droplets. Vlad ducked, but several drops fell on his exposed skin. He shook his arm wildly in the air, but then he wondered why it wasn't burning, or even making him slightly nauseated. Vlad sniffed his skin and breathed a sigh of relief. It wasn't garlic juice after all.

For a moment Joss's eyes were wide, horrified.

Vlad plucked the vial from the ground. The worn label read HOLY WATER. Vlad shook his head but couldn't manage so much as a chuckle. He tossed the vial back on the ground and faced Joss—his friend, his enemy. "Just so you know, the cross won't work either. They're myths—kinda like how all vampires are evil."

Joss gripped the stake in his hand and held it up in Vlad's line of sight. "But this will."

With his heart pounding out a quick beat, Vlad dared to step closer. "You think you know so much about me, about those like me. But you don't. You just think we're mindless, heartless monsters. But we aren't. We're people, Joss. With family, friends, ideas, lives! Just like humans, there are bad vampires." He glanced at D'Ablo. "But we're not all like that. I'm not like that."

"You think you're the only one betrayed here, Vlad? You're lying to everyone! No one in Bathory knows what a killer you are!" Joss lowered the stake, as if he were intent on ramming it up under Vlad's ribs.

Anger boiled up from within Vlad, and he snatched the stake from Joss's hand and threw it to the ground. The silver tip stuck in the soft soil. "How can you be my friend one minute and my enemy the next? That's not right! It's not fair! Vampire or not, I'm the same person I was yesterday, the same friend you asked to come with you tonight. I haven't changed, Joss. Why have you?" Tears threatened to roll from his eyes, but Vlad tried hard to keep them contained. "I'm not a killer."

Joss's eyes were locked on Vlad's. His voice shook with a whisper. "I've never seen purple eyes before. Not even on a vampire. What kind of monster are you?"

Vlad paused for a moment, taken aback by Joss's tone. He sounded awed, but mostly, he sounded scared. Vlad blinked, knowing his eyes had changed to that strange iridescent purple once again.

He glanced at D'Ablo and Jasik, who had stepped back to watch the show. D'Ablo looked enormously pleased, for some reason.

The anger left Vlad in a rush, and he looked at his friend with a pleading gaze. "You don't have to do this. You wouldn't be killing a monster; you'd be murdering a friend. Please . . . don't."

Joss dropped his gaze to the stake. A tear rolled down his cheek and dripped to the ground.

"I know it's been tough moving around, trying to make new friends. Well, you've made one in me, Joss. We're friends." Vlad knew he could push into Joss's mind to see what he was thinking, but he didn't really want to know. Instead, he watched . . . and waited.

"Kill him." D'Ablo's voice was stern and gruff.

Vlad backed up quickly, forgetting about Joss for a moment. Jasik appeared out of nowhere, grabbed him by the arms, and held him still. Vlad yanked his body forward, breaking free. He broke into a run toward the trees.

But he stopped dead in his tracks.

In his mind were images of D'Ablo and Jasik feeding on every drop of blood that Joss carried. But he hadn't put them there. The thoughts were coming from someone else. Vlad looked at D'Ablo, who nodded. If Vlad ran, they'd kill Joss, and then come after him. He couldn't let that happen. Joss was his friend—even if he did have some pretty messed-up ideas about vampires.

D'Ablo's voice was crisp. "It doesn't have to be that way, Vladimir. Your friend needn't suffer."

Vlad ran his tongue over his protruding fangs. He had no idea they'd elongated. "Otis will avenge my death. You have no idea the hurt that's coming for you if I die."

D'Ablo tilted his head. The smile on his lips was almost endearing. "I'm willing to take that chance."

The air left Vlad's lungs. His stomach cramped. From behind him, he thought he heard Joss whisper, "For you, Cecile." But he couldn't be sure. It felt as though he'd been punched very hard in the back. Time slowed to a crawl.

Vlad turned his head as he dropped to his knees. Joss was standing behind him, troubled, but triumphant. Vlad took a deep breath, feeling hot liquid bubble inside his chest. He tried another breath, but the air wouldn't come.

D'Ablo was kneeling in front of him, watching Vlad's chest with enormous interest. Vlad looked down—it felt as if it took hours just to make the effort. A spike of silver gleamed at his center. Vlad reached up and touched it.

The stake. Joss had staked him.

Vlad blinked. His eyes were heavy, but he forced them open. His clothes were soaked with something that made his stomach rumble. It almost made him laugh, but then Vlad coughed, and a searing pain ripped through his chest. He looked back at Joss. Jasik was stepping closer to him.

Vlad coughed again, but despite his pain, he didn't cry. He parted his bloodstained lips and managed a whisper. "Joss. Behind . . ."

But the air was gone. Joss was gone. The clearing, the vampires, the trees, the sky—all disappeared in a swirl of black. In Vlad's last semiconscious thought, he wished that Joss would get away from Jasik and D'Ablo . . . and that Otis would avenge his death.

He tried once more to breathe, to no avail.

22

THE AFTERLIFE

VLAD TUMBLED FORWARD into the black oblivion of death.
It felt strange to die. At first, it seemed like he was falling, but then he felt like he was being lifted up by many
hands. There was a *GUSH* sensation in his chest, and suddenly, Vlad could breathe. In the darkness of his mind, he
saw Otis's face—grim, determined, sorrowful. Vikas's voice
invaded his thoughts. "Be Still, Mahlyenki Dyavol."

And Vlad was still.

After minutes, hours, days—Vlad couldn't be sure which—
lights pierced the darkness. Blue and red. They appeared in
circles and brought with them the wailing of a banshee. *This
is it, then*, Vlad thought. *I've died and this is what the afterlife*

is like. He thought there were supposed to be harps, pearly gates, and people flying around with big, feathery wings. But there was none of that. Only pain and darkness, with the occasional odd sound and weird, colored lights—what a gyp.

Vlad took a deep breath and ignored the weird slapping sound coming from his chest. Otis's face loomed once more above him. Vlad began to speak, to warn his uncle about D'Ablo and Joss, but a wave of blackness dragged him back under.

He floated there in a haze for a long time, just below the edge of consciousness. When he surfaced again, it was to Nelly's voice. Only he couldn't make out what she was saying through her sobbing. He tried to tell her he'd miss her but couldn't manage to open his mouth.

Time moved again, and Vlad returned to his haze. Voices kept him company, though he didn't recognize most of them. After what seemed like an eternity, Vlad forced his eyes open. His eyelids felt heavy with sleep, but he saw that he was lying on a crisp white bed. A tube stuck out of his hand. It led up a long silver pole to a clear bag, marked with colored stickers. One of the stickers read MORPHINE. Another tube stuck out of his other hand—this one led to a bag of blood.

No wonder he wasn't hungry.

And he was alive! His heart ached, but it was beating. His lungs burned, but they were breathing. His body hurt all over . . . but he lived. He'd survived, somehow.

He wanted to thank whoever had brought him here, to hug someone—anyone—and tell them he loved them, to see Nelly and Otis and Henry again. And if he ever managed to get out of the hospital, he was going to take Meredith Brookstone to the Freedom Fest dance again, and afterward, he was going to give her a kiss that she'd never forget.

He was alive. Impossibly, he was alive.

And he was in the hospital . . . where doctors and nurses would surely notice his hunger for blood and his sharp-as-razors fangs.

Vlad turned his head, feeling less heavy, and looked at the nurse, who was checking the graph that was being printed by machine next to his bed. His lips were dry when he parted them to speak. "Where am I?"

The nurse looked up at him with surprised eyes. "You're in Stokerton General Hospital. Are you in pain?"

Vlad licked his lips. "No. Just thirsty."

Without a word, the nurse moved out the door. When she returned a moment later, she had a cup of water. Vlad sipped it slowly through the straw. He cleared his throat and asked, "Is my aunt here?"

The nurse smiled and patted his arm. "She just stepped out for a moment. I believe your uncle is in the waiting room. Would you like me to get him for you?"

Vlad blinked. "Otis is here?"

Without answering or waiting for Vlad's reply, the nurse disappeared out the door again, leaving Vlad alone in his hospital room.

On a small panel to his left there were several buttons. Vlad tried a few until he found the one to help him sit up. After he did, he lifted the sheet and noted with great disgust that he was wearing one of those ugly blue-checkered hospital gowns. With any luck, the nurse who dressed him had been male, but Vlad doubted it. He ran a hand gently over his chest and noted the lump of bandages wrapped snugly around him.

In the hall, he heard someone running, followed shortly by a warning from one of the staff. Vlad's door flew open, revealing a very relieved-looking Otis. When he met Vlad's eyes, he sighed. "Thank goodness. I thought you might not make it."

Vlad winced at the pain in his chest. "That makes two of us."

Otis closed the door behind him and moved to Vlad's side. "How do you feel?"

Relieved. Relieved he was looking once again at his uncle's face, after he'd already said in his mind good-bye to Otis forever. That was the first thing that came to mind, but he didn't say it. Vlad choked back tears but tried hard to keep his voice calm. "Tired. But otherwise, okay. The nurse said Nelly is here."

Otis nodded and cast a longing glance at Vlad's blood bag. His eyes look sunk in, as if he hadn't eaten in days.

"She and Henry just stepped out for some lunch. They'll be back momentarily."

The calming effect of the morphine released Vlad for a moment and he clutched Otis's hand. "Uncle Otis, D'Ablo's alive. I don't know how. He drank some of my blood. And . . . Joss . . ."

Otis held up a hand. "We know everything, Vladimir. I'm just ashamed we couldn't get there in time."

"Joss staked me. He's the slayer." Vlad fought back tears at the memory.

Otis's forehead creased. "We know."

"We?"

Otis offered a nod. "Vikas and I. The moment I received your letter about Jasik's attack, I boarded a plane for the Americas. But I was arrested in France by the Parisian council. Vikas managed to aid in my escape from Elysia just days ago, after he obtained proof that D'Ablo was still very much alive. We were in the car and minutes from Bathory when I heard your telepathic cry for help. We each tried to reach you, but D'Ablo must have been blocking your mind after that. I suspect a Tego charm but can't be certain."

Tears escaped Otis's eyes. "When I saw you there, with that hunk of wood sticking out of your back, and all that blood . . ." He swallowed hard. "I just never thought I'd get the chance to teach you all of the things that I want; to show you all that I can. There's so much I have to tell you, so much time I want to spend with you."

Vlad took a deep breath and coughed some at the odd tickle in his chest. "I've never been to the hospital before. Won't they know I'm . . . different?"

Otis dried his eyes. "It took us a while to convince Nelly that you had to come to the hospital in Stokerton. We have doctors on staff here, nurses, too. You're under their care right now, so as not to raise suspicions."

Vlad blinked. "So that nurse . . . ?"

"One of our kind, yes."

There was a soft knock on the door, and then it swung open, revealing Vikas. He was still wearing his fur jacket, and on his brow glistened small beads of sweat. "It is warm here in your country, Vladimir."

Vlad smiled. "Yeah, you might wanna lose that coat."

As Vikas was slipping off his jacket, Vlad glanced at Otis. "When Jasik bit me, I felt really strange. Hot, dizzy, heavy. But I didn't feel like that at all when you gave me my mark. Was it because Jasik was trying to kill me?"

A strange silence fell over the room for several moments. Then, clearing his throat, Otis said, "No, Vladimir. Jasik wasn't trying to kill you—that would be against Elysian law. How-ever, just as some vampires believe that the blood of the Pravus has great healing capabilities, some believe that if you were to drink enough of his blood, you could strengthen yourself completely against sunlight. Likely, Jasik believes that you are the Pravus. Or perhaps he drank so much just in case you were."

Vlad thought about the healed hole in D'Ablo's stomach and emitted a shuddering sigh. He wet his lips. "So, what happened to Joss?"

Otis and Vikas exchanged glances before Otis said, "By the time we arrived at the clearing in Bathory, having searched the town, we found you on the ground, slumped over. Joss was standing over you, his hands covered in your blood. D'Ablo and Jasik were nowhere in sight. Vikas checked your pulse."

Vikas laid his jacket on a nearby chair. "It was very weak, but you were still alive. Your uncle examined you closer while I questioned the boy. He said nothing, but his thoughts gave away his crime. I offered to destroy him, but Otis refused me the pleasure. Instead, Nelly took him back to her home and telephoned an ambulance. She was very upset."

Otis nodded gravely. "Vikas and I decided to take what precautions we could. I held you while he pulled the stake out. Then I cut my wrist and gave you as much blood as I could bear to."

Vlad's eyes welled with tears at Otis's generosity. He shook his head. "But how did I survive? I mean, fairy tales aside, shouldn't a stake through the heart kill just about any living thing?"

Again, Otis and Vikas exchanged glances. But this time, neither opted to reply.

Vlad looked at each of them for a moment before speaking. "What? He did miss my heart; otherwise we wouldn't be having this conversation."

Otis glanced at the floor and then back at Vikas before meeting Vlad's eyes. "It's possible he missed your heart and pierced a lung, but with as fast as you were healing after I put my wrist to your mouth . . . there's no way to tell for sure."

Vlad looked at Vikas and found no question in his eyes. He looked back at his uncle. "You do think I'm the Pravus, don't you?"

Otis's face grew white at the word, but he didn't speak.

"Otis." Vlad's voice cracked. "Look at me."

After a moment of hesitation, his uncle complied.

"Do you believe I'm the Pravus?"

Otis closed a hand over Vlad's. An intense hope flickered in his eyes. "I believe that one day you will be a great man, Vladimir. And that prophecies and heritage count for nothing—it is our actions that decide what kind of men we are." He squeezed Vlad's hand, determination set in his jaw. "Let your actions speak to the world, Vlad."

Vlad nodded, unable to speak.

Vikas squeezed Otis's shoulder. Otis looked at him and gave an assenting nod, as if they were carrying on a conversation that Vlad couldn't hear. Otis looked once more to Vlad and cleared his throat—the fear still lingering in his gaze. "I'll go call Nelly. She'll want to see you right away."

Vlad swallowed the lump in his throat. "What about D'Ablo?"

Otis paused with his hand on the door and cleared his throat. "He's returned to Elysia to continue his presidency."

Vlad couldn't speak. And if he'd been able to, he wouldn't have. Some moments call for silence.

After Otis left the room, Vikas closed the door and turned back to Vlad. His dark eyes were brooding. "The boy is here. He wants to speak with you."

Vlad furrowed his brow. "Joss?" His hand went instinctively to his bandaged chest.

Vikas nodded. "I will stay in the room to prevent incident."

Vlad shook his head. He didn't need a babysitter or a guard. Joss, despite all this, was Vlad's friend. But when Vikas looked at Vlad, Vlad knew there would be no convincing him of the friendship he'd shared with the slayer. He took a sip of his water and sat it down on the table next to his bed. "When can I see him?"

Vikas stood very still, eyeing Vlad, as if there were something he wanted to share with him. But when Vlad raised an eyebrow at his Russian friend. Vikas merely moved to the door and opened it without saying a word.

Joss was standing out in the hall, staring intently at the floor between his feet. He walked into the room with hardly an upward glance. Vikas closed the door and stood protectively behind Joss until Vlad shook his head. Then Vikas chose a seat nearest Joss. It would have to do.

Vlad kept his tone clipped. The guy *did* stab him in the chest after all. "Why are you here, Joss?"

Joss looked up at Vlad but only for a moment. "Not to apologize, if that's what you're expecting."

Vlad pursed his lips together. "You tried to kill me and you can't even manage a feeble 'I'm sorry'? Don't you think I deserve at least that?"

Joss shook his head. The floor had apparently lost its interest, as he was looking into Vlad's eyes. "It wouldn't mean anything, because I wouldn't mean it."

"You don't have to mean it, Joss." Vlad took a breath—not too deep, as the pressure of the bandages prevented him from doing so—and quieted his tone. "But it would be nice to hear. At least pretend you care that I'm lying in a hospital."

Joss winced. His eyes grew moist, but no tears fell. "I do care."

Vlad met Joss's gaze. "Then why? Why did you do it? Money? Sport? Because I'm a monster?"

"Because it's my job, Vlad." A tear betrayed Joss's stern expression and rolled down his cheek. It hung briefly from his jaw before letting go and free-falling to the floor.

"You know virtually nothing about us, Joss. You fear what you don't understand, and you react violently to what it is you fear. Have you ever thought of getting educated on the people you're killing? Don't you think you owe them that much?" The tickle in Vlad's chest returned. He almost coughed but managed to suppress it.

Joss's eyes were no longer shimmering. "Who am I supposed to learn from—one of you? My beliefs have been passed down to me from generation to generation. Centuries of knowledge and opinion."

"Did you ever once try to think for yourself?" Vlad glared. His fangs threatened to push out of his gums at the scent of Joss's blood pulsing through his veins, but he willed them to remain hidden. "I'm just lucky you missed and hit a lung. Why exactly did you come here? To finish the job, maybe?"

Joss glanced at Vikas. "With your bodyguard here, that would be incredibly stupid of me, wouldn't it?"

Vlad smirked. "You gotta admit, it's pretty stupid for an unarmed slayer to enter a closed room with two vampires, wouldn't you say?"

Vikas's deep laughter rolled through the room.

Joss slanted his eyes at Vlad. "Who says I'm unarmed?"

Vikas's laughter ceased immediately. He stood and took a step closer to Joss before Vlad held up a hand to stop him.

The room was quiet for many minutes.

"Listen," Vlad began. "Watch out for D'Ablo. He's devious, evil—gives vampires a bad name, the way I understand it. You should be careful. Take whatever protective measures you can."

Joss tilted his head. "Why are you telling me this?"

Vlad's voice cracked. His cheeks were moist before he realized he was going to cry. "Because you're my friend."

Joss's bottom lip trembled until he bit it back into submission. He turned to the door. His fingers had just brushed the handle when he glanced back at Vlad. "I came here to tell you I'm going back to Santa Carla."

Vlad furrowed his brow. "What about finishing your job here?"

Joss shook his head. "The Slayer Society didn't send me here, remember? It was a private job. As far as they know, and as far as I'm telling them . . . there are no vampires in Bathory." Joss held Vlad's gaze for a moment, then pushed the door open and stepped through it. He paused and glanced back over his shoulder. "By the way, I may have nicked a lung, but I didn't miss. I never miss."

Vlad pressed the button on the bed panel until he was lying down. Hot tears rolled from his eyes to the pillowcase.

There was no doubt now. He couldn't fight it any longer. He was the Pravus, after all.

Vikas moved closer. "Are you in pain, Little Devil?"

Vlad shook his head slowly.

Vikas sighed. "The worst pain in the world goes beyond the physical. Even further beyond any other emotional pain one can feel. It is in the betrayal of a friend."

Vlad closed his eyes, and despite his effort not to cry, more tears escaped.

"I have been betrayed as well by a friend, Vladimir. Perhaps one day we shall share these tales of pain and find a moment of laughter in them."

Vlad gave up his effort and let the tears come. He wished that Vikas would leave him alone, so he could get all the pain out by crying into his pillow, but it seemed Vikas refused to leave.

Vikas was quiet for a moment, and then he said, "You should rest. Your aunt will be here soon, and no rest will come when there is mothering to be done."

Vlad swore he could hear the smile in Vikas's tone. It was followed by the click of the light switch and a closing door.

Vlad clutched his bandaged chest and cried.

Though Vlad couldn't recall having slipped away into unconsciousness, he must have slept for a while, because when he opened his eyes again, they were crusty with sleep. He reached up and rubbed the crunchy gunk away. The only sound in the room was the heart monitor to his left that blipped and beeped occasionally. He hovered his finger over the nurse's button, but the door to his room opened, so he relaxed his hand.

Nelly stepped in, wearing tear-smeared mascara with dark circles under her eyes. When she saw Vlad, she started crying again and hugged him. Vlad hugged her back and nudged her gently away from his shoulder so that he could understand what she was saying through her sobs. "You're okay. Otis said you would be, but I just didn't know. I thought . . . I thought I'd lost you!" She buried her face in her hands again, and Vlad hugged her close and let her cry.

He fought the tears but lost, weeping softly into Nelly's shoulder for everything to be normal again. For all the pain and loss that he'd suffered from, that they'd suffered from, to be gone. At last his tears subsided, and he tried to sit back in a more comfortable position, but Nelly clung to him.

Vikas held the door open for Otis, who managed to coax Nelly away from Vlad after several minutes and substitute his own shoulder. Henry was in the hall, a bandage on his forehead, looking more than a little concerned. His eyes were puffy and red. With a shaking sigh, Henry entered the room and closed the door behind him. His expression shifted from upset to relieved when he met Vlad's gaze.

Vlad smiled. He wanted to say something to ease their tension, to take away their sorrow, but he couldn't think of anything, so he merely shrugged and asked, "So when can I go home?"

Over Nelly's sobs, Otis said, "The doctors say a month, at the least. Despite how quickly you heal."

Vlad sighed. "And how long will you be staying, Otis?"

Otis met his gaze. A glimmer of determination crossed his eyes. "Until late summer. And then I'm going to go find the ritual passage D'Ablo is so desperate for. After all, without it, your life is safe."

Vlad nodded, relieved Otis was staying for at least a little while, and pursed his lips, trying hard to push down the anger and sadness that he was feeling, but they refused to leave him, so he lay back and closed his eyes again.

"Don't you think you've slept enough?" Henry was next to his bed, and probably wearing a smirk.

Vlad opened his eyes. Sure enough, Henry was smiling. After a second, so was Vlad. "I'll sleep when I'm dead."

Nelly shot him a wide-eyed look. "Vladimir! That's not funny!"

Vlad grinned. "Okay, so I'll sleep when I'm undead."

Henry didn't miss his cue. "Too late."

Otis calmed Nelly's protests by leading her out the door with promises of hot coffee, and Vikas followed, after exchanging smiles with Vlad and his rather amusing drudge.

After they were gone, Henry said, "Well, if the stake-through-the-heart stereotype isn't true, I wonder what else is a myth. I mean, where's your superhuman strength?"

"Don't lose hope." Vlad chuckled and winced at the pain in his chest.

Vlad pointed to the bandage on Henry's head. "What happened?"

Henry's fingers found the bandage, and he frowned. "Oh, that. It was the weirdest thing. I got this feeling, like I should find you, like you were going to be in trouble soon if I didn't. And this guy came outta nowhere and clocked me over the head. I woke up a few hours later and just knew you'd been hurt. Your uncle said that that Jasik guy had taken me temporarily out of commission, something about getting your drudge out of the way long enough to get a stake into you."

"Holy crap, Henry." Vlad shook his head in astonishment. Apparently, D'Ablo and Jasik had all the little details ironed out.

Henry took on a more serious tone. "So about Joss . . ."

Vlad glanced at the door. "I don't want to talk about him, Henry. In fact, I'd rather forget the whole thing ever happened."

Henry nodded, and the room fell silent for a moment. Then, in an act of complete normalcy, Henry grinned and said, "Hey, did you see the cute nurse out in the hall?"

23

THE SILVER LINING

VLAD SHIFTED HIS backpack to a more comfortable spot on his back and followed Henry through the double doors of Bathory High. Spring had been flirting heavily with summer during the last week of school; so the staff had turned on fans to try to keep the peace. It hadn't worked—the fans just whirred loudly, giving everyone headaches and messing up their hair without really cooling them off. And nothing is more unpleasant than a few hundred teenagers forced to study algebraic equations while sweat beads on their skin.

Vlad hadn't felt much like talking since he left the hospital. Henry had asked repeatedly for the details of Joss's attack—always on the heels of apologizing for his cousin's actions—but Vlad wasn't feeling up to sharing just yet. Pretty much, he wanted to put the ordeal behind him and get back to the usual stuff, like hanging out with Henry the way they had before Joss had shown up in their quaint little town. It's funny how getting stabbed through the heart by a friend can bring your whole school year down. He was lucky that Nelly had convinced his teachers to let him advance to tenth grade next year, despite so many missed tests. The homework he'd caught up on, though, so apparently his grades weren't as bad as they could have been. Right now, though, he was looking forward to summer vacation.

Vlad turned his head and looked at Joss's locker, now empty. He hadn't seen Joss since that day in the hospital. By the time he got home, Joss had split town, thankfully without revealing Vlad's secret to anyone. As far as Vlad knew, he hadn't even mentioned it to Henry. Joss might be an attempted murderer and the worst kind of backstabber imaginable, but at least he was a man of his word.

Henry squeezed Vlad's shoulder. They'd both lost a good friend that day.

Then Vlad saw it. Taped to his locker was a parchment envelope, closed with a red wax seal bearing the initials *S.S.* Slayer Society. He pulled the flap open and withdrew a small sheet of parchment. On it, in Joss's handwriting, was a single, short phrase, written in stark, black ink: FRIEND-SHIP OVER.

Vlad took a shuddered breath and tucked the note back into the envelope.

Henry closed his own locker and was fiddling with the lock. Vlad watched him without interest. Eddie Poe passed by and offered Vlad a glare—apparently near-death experiences aren't enough to get the media off of your back. The Eddie situation was something he'd have to deal with eventually, but for now, just knowing Joss wasn't around to hurt him anymore was enough. More than anything, Vlad just wanted his freshman year to be over. Not that he expected his sophomore year to be much better, especially if Eddie didn't get over his monster obsession . . . but hey, a guy can dream.

"Vlad?"

Vlad's grip on his backpack strap tightened. He turned around and for a moment, forgot how to form coherent words. Strange how a pretty girl's face can render you speechless.

Meredith smiled. "I was just wondering if I'd see you at Freedom Fest tonight."

Her hair was tied up in a ponytail, adorned with a pink satin ribbon. Vlad had to concentrate to keep from reaching up and running his hand over her silken tresses. He managed a smile. "Of course. Are you . . . are you going to the dance with anyone?"

The blush in Meredith's cheeks deepened a shade. "That depends on you."

Henry took his cue and moved down the hall to first period. Vlad dropped his backpack in his locker and retrieved his books for his first two classes. He shut the door and took a deep breath, letting it out slowly. "How about I walk you to class and we can talk about it some more?"

"Actually, I'm helping out in the library first hour."

Vlad smiled. "Then I'll walk you to the library."

Meredith's small smile broke into a grin. Vlad took her books for her, and they moved down the hall. As they walked, their hands found each other. Vlad's heart, once again healthy and strong, beat against his ribs in one continuous rhythm. When they reached the library, he gave her hand a gentle squeeze. She squeezed his, and as they parted, their fingertips lingered to touch.

Meredith's voice was hushed in the nearly empty hallway. "Will I see you after class?"

Vlad beamed. "Count on it."

The door closed behind Meredith, and Vlad floated down the hall to first-period English. Tonight was Freedom Fest, and this time, he was going to make Meredith happy she went with him.

Check out the next chapter in:

THE CHRONICLES OF
Vladimir Tod

TENTH GRADE
BLEEDS

1
HUNTER FOR HIRE

IGNATIUS DREW THE CURVED BLADE along the whetstone slowly, the gritty sound filling his ears. It had to be sharp, sharp enough to slice into bone if necessary. He didn't expect to kill the halfling boy, only to damage him, break him, before dragging his nearly lifeless body before the council, as he'd been hired to do. But if the boy gave him any trouble at all, Ignatius would take his bloody pleasures slowly, so that the boy felt every bruise, every cut.

He almost hoped the boy would fight back, give him an excuse to torture him. After all, he had it coming. His very existence was an abomination.

Small sparks flew from the blade, and at last, Ignatius pulled metal from stone. He ran his thumb along the steel, splitting his pale skin open. Blood—rich, red—dripped from the cut before it healed closed again.

He was hungry. It was always better to hunt when he was hungry. He hadn't eaten in months, in eager anticipation of that insatiable need pushing him through the capture and, perhaps, the kill.

The council had been clear: "Bring us Vladimir Tod and your reward will be immeasurable." They never mentioned in what condition to bring him, had only barely stressed that he should be living. Little did they know, Ignatius didn't require payment. Causing the boy's suffering—and perhaps even his death, he thought with a pleasant shiver—would be reward enough.

The boy who would be the Pravus. The thought enraged Ignatius further, and he returned his blade to the whetstone, working it slowly, smoothing the edge into a razor.

Soon. Once the final paperwork was signed, his hunt would begin.

And Vladimir Tod would be made to suffer.